COME THE KINGDOM

A Novel by

HEATHER H. COEN

eBook ISBN: 978-1-965761-04-5
Paperback ISBN: 978-1-965761-05-2
Ingram Spark ISBN: 978-1-965761-06-9

Editor: Carol Koppleman, Sally Roberts
Cover Image: Original Painting by Heather H. Coen
Original Painting in book: Heather H. Coen
Cover Design: Angie Ayala
Interior Design: Marigold2k
Publisher: Spotlight Publishing House™
https://SpotlightPublishingHouse.com

Table of Contents

1. The Casting 1
2. Silkies 7
3. Patmos Islands 9
4. Retrieved 11
5. Krushe 17
6. Recuperation 35
7. Palace of Thieves 37
8. Crossings 45
9. The Pass 59
10. The Guards at the Gate 75
11. Returned 91
12. Plans Mature 123
13. River Chebar 169
14. From Chaos 175
15. Homeward Bound 185
16. Travelers 201
17. Freedom Indeed 207
Glossary 215
About the Author 219

DEDICATED TO...

My late husband and life partner, Richard W. Coen.

To those who have held me up in times of great need:

Marti and Don Denham
Susanne Mills
Debbie Peterson

RIEL RAN AGAM

A Novel by Heather H. Coen

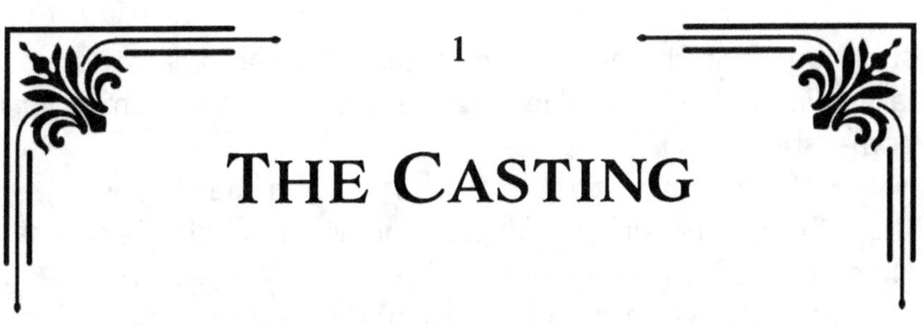

THE CASTING

My dear brothers and sisters, take note of this:
Everyone should be quick to listen,
slow to speak and slow to become angry.
James 1:19-20

As the sun set, casting its final rays on the churning sea, the evening star emerged in the black, moonless sky. High on a bleached white bluff, the cry of a newborn baby echoed, signaling a profound change in the world.

A falling star shot through the sky in wild abandon of crimson, blue and viridian. Short lived, the meteor's last embers died as the atmosphere ate its bones to nothing.

In the morning as the mists cleared, the baby's mother rocked him, crooning in her sweet high voice. Her song rang across the clear sea air. She held the baby in a clutch of rags. Her own clothing, though once rich and fine, had degraded into the same rotted material. But no apparel could take away from her stunning face - almond shaped wide blue eyes as clear as the sea's water on a crystal day, dark slanting brows, and porcelain skin: Hers was the face of a queen.

However, her mouth was what men starred at as her lips were ruby red and her faultless white teeth were as brilliant as fresh snow on a winter day. She had gotten bone thin running as she had for the last seven months, her horse lost the previous day. But her face was set with grim determination. She had finally made the Western Sea at the very edge of the Carmel Coasts, but it was her final and last hope. She did not expect the baby boy to come as early as he had and for herself to be so brutally hungry. She walked down the cliff path to the shore and held the baby to her breast. She sat exhausted on a large piece of driftwood letting the sun warm her. Liam would come, she knew it.

Her feet were warmed in the sand, and she slipped down the driftwood nestling in a depression with her baby held close. He cooed softly and opened his brilliant blue eyes. She began to weep and fell into weary depleted, slumber. A few hours later a shadow crossed her peaceful face, and she suddenly woke. The sun behind his back and head, Liam reached down and helped her up.

She had physically seen him only three times in her life but lived day to day hanging onto his spiritual presence. It was a very rare event that he took on form and body. He looked at her with love and approval shining in his eyes.

Liam was tall and thin; he had a plain face really with a somewhat uneven quality about it. His curly hair was dark auburn, and he wore it in braid flowing down his back; more escaped than was contained in the plait leaving winding curls framing his honest face. His eyes were as dark as the night skies yet filled with such light that many could not look in them for any length of time. His brows were lighter than his hair, fanning out to frame his dark eyes; his nose was long and narrow but flared to a nice, upturned tip; a series of small scars marred a narrow strip across his wide forehead. His lips were unremarkable, but his porcelain teeth were perfect and when he spoke it was soft and gentle but somehow had impact and clarity.

He said simply, "He has your eyes beloved Ariel. I have brought you a few things to eat so you have the strength to finish." He handed her a piece of cheese, an orange and a large piece of bread soaked in herbed butter. She sat back down on the driftwood and carefully tasted and ate the food. He held the baby and watched her carefully.

Liam said, "You understand that it is time, and he must be parted from you. You were aware of the cost when you conceived him with Aran. The Prophecy was brought to you and the King by the saints and prophets I sent. You knew it would cost your life and only a few brief hours with your baby."

A tear slipped down her dirt-stained cheek and Ariel cried out: "Lord I am loath to leave my first-born baby only twenty-hours old." Her beautiful face twisted in agony as she retrieved the child and tenderly touched the baby's cheek.

He replied, "Ariel you have been incredibly brave. You have managed to stay ahead of the minions for seven months and given birth all alone. Now you're giving up your only child with the enemy right at the gate. By your sacrifice, you have saved your son's life and your Kingdom from years of slavery and the lives of so many others. I am giving you this knife. Hide it in your clothes and deal a last blow to Aragant. Today you will meet me in Paradise, and I will be there waiting for you."

She bent and kissed her son's tiny lips, looking with love and regret into her child's handsome face. Then she turned to Liam and stood against his body hugging him to her with the baby. She kissed Liam on the cheek. She handed him the baby and turned away, walking toward the towering white cliffs. It was very hard not to look back. Not to think about her life so close to ending and her baby gone. She would have been thirty years old the following summer.

Just a few minutes later, she heard a horse's harness jingling above her on the cliff. She ran hoping to hide in a cleft. It was too late; he had already spotted her. It was only a few minutes before the guards found the route down, their dark hearts thirsting for her blood.

She was caught running across a strand of sand and they roughly hoisted her between two horses. She twisted and fought the guards, but she was at the limit of her strength.

Aragant stood on the beach, waiting for his men to deliver her. Revenge covered every pore of his skin, seeping foul venom into his soul. He had waited seven long months for this moment, crossing half a continent and draining his resources. But he had her at last! His silver jeweled collar glistened in the morning sun as he rubbed his palms together in anticipation. The soldiers threw the Queen down in front of him.

He walked around her crumpled form, his spiked boots leaving heel impressions in the sand.

"Well, we are united at last my Queen after all these many months of chase. And see, you grovel before me as it should be." He took a moment to polish the blade on his knife before he looked at her.

She looked up, sand covering her face as she wiped tears from her eyes. She was beaten at last but the blazing look in her eyes told Aragant she was not defeated yet. She pulled a lock of her black hair away from her scratched and bruising face.

"You are too late, you evil incompetent idiot," said the Queen with loathing in her voice. "You will be surprised to learn all is not as you think, for where is the baby you so desperately wanted to kill? I have won in the end and there is nothing you can do to stop the Prophecy now. It doesn't matter what you do to me."

He was tempted to hit her with his riding crop, but he hesitated, wondering what she meant about winning and then he realized she was no longer pregnant. Where was the little brat? She had eluded him for months even being heavy with a child. The silver in his saddle bags was down to a few coins with the payments he had made to maintain her trail. And now, when victory was his, she is captured after giving birth and there was no sign of the child anywhere. Perhaps the thing was female and not even worth this pursuit.

Aragant raised his hand to her and was about to strike her spitting out the words, "So my witch Queen, where is your child?"

"He is well away from your minions," she replied with hatred coloring her voice. As forceful as she tried to sound, it came out low pitched and hardly audible for want of water.

Aragant realized she needed water as he could hardly hear her reply. He had to know if the brat survived as he had run her ragged in his pursuit. She was so thin; he was surprised she was still alive. Still, she was beautiful beyond almost description even with her gaunt cheekbones. He walked to his horse and retrieved his canteen and handed it to her.

In a swift unexpected move, she stood pretending to reach for the canteen but instead, in one fluid movement, removed Liam's knife from her pocket and slashed across Aragant's face, making a gash from his cheek all the way up to his forehead. A flow of blood coursed down his cheek as the anger reached through his soul to her.

He quickly responded with fury and with many years of training, his scimitar was in his hand and with all his strength he stabbed her through her chest, the point protruding through her back. She fell to the ground, with a pool of maroon draining into the hungry sands.

She turned her contorted face towards him, and said, "No torture and the baby will never be found now. The Lord has won, and the Prophecy is assured." Blood gurgled through her lips, and she let out a final ragged breath.

He bent down on one knee and stabbed her five more times even though her life had slipped away. He cursed himself for not keeping her bound and alive until he had the information he needed. This would not set well when he returned to the palace. His men spent the next five days searching the beaches and cliffs for any sign of the baby but there was nothing but a few blood-stained cloths on the cliff top.

SILKIES

*"So, God created great sea creatures
and every sort of fish, and every kind of bird."*
Genesis 1:21

O ut in the waves two Silkies rushed to the mainland shores. Liam's call had come, and they knew the time of the Prophecy was upon them. Relinquishing their seal skins to become human women had not happened in many years. These were two older Silkies and their life exceeded men by many years.

Deep in a cove, three miles from where Ariel's blood was draining into the shifting sands, The Horns of the Kings was being blown. Aragant's men heard the long low sounds of the horns and their hair raised on their necks. Their horses cried out, stomping the sand as the sound came three times knelling the death of Queen Ariel Agam.

The Silkies reached the shore and stood naked before Liam, their long-curled hair twisting around their perfectly shaped women's bodies. He simply handed Riel Ran Agam to Liberty, the first Silkie and the baby opened his brilliant eyes to both Silkies.

Liberty asked, "Is he ours to keep?"

"Is there ever a child that is not the gift of God?" said Liam. "He is yours to teach the ways of the seas, but I warn you I will come again to retrieve him when he is needed. He is the child of Adriel Agam the Queen. She has sacrificed all for him and even now her blood is being collected from the sands where it was spilled. Soon the otters will bring you a vial of it. When I call, you must return him to me, along with the vial."

Freeborn, the second Silkie, asked, "Are we to teach him the secrets of the deep?"

"You must never let him touch or see another human until I come for him," replied Liam. "You must teach him the Ocean Speech, language of the humans, and the deep's secrets. He must never be left unguarded by you or the otters until I come for him. He is not to be handed or trusted to anyone else. Be careful that you do not allow anger to color your thoughts towards the child and never let it dwell in you past sunset. You must restrict him to your three islands. You must pray with him every single day and let him go with the otters from time to time."

Freeborn said, "Lord there are only two of us! The islands are passed by many ships, what will we do?"

The Lord smiled, pointing out to the water beyond the crashing waves where three otters, twenty-five seals, a walrus and a Minke Whale swam. Their heads bobbed up and down, all of them looking at the Silkies. "It takes a village to raise a child or in this case a pod or school," replied Liam with a smile curling on his lips. He rotated a large piece of driftwood to Liberty which had a depressed bowl in the center just the right size for a baby cradle.

PATMOS
ISLANDS

I was exiled to the island of Patmos...
Revelation 1:9

The Silkies put the baby in the driftwood and floated it out into the waves. They returned to their seal forms gently pushing the wood towards the Patmos Islands some distance offshore. He began to cry just as they approached land. The sea birds plunged and dove from the cliffs above as the Silkies pushed the craft into a cave hidden inside a cliff and covered in shadowing vines. They slid up a small ramp onto a rock platform a few feet above the water and reverted to human form as they cautiously lifted the child from the wood and removed the rags he was wrapped in.

On a shelf in the cave the Silkies had gathered clothing, linens, and blankets as well as items the baby would need over the coming months. In the past three years four ships had sunk offshore and the plunder somewhat miraculously washed up on the islands. Nothing had reached their shores before, never mind the items needed for a small child.

Soon a seal appeared, and she waded onto the rock platform. She turned to the side and the Silkies dried her off, put Riel in a couple of blankets and nestled him next to her teat. He soon got the idea with a little help. The Silkies discussed his care with the seal carefully telling her she could not move while he suckled. Soon the babe was sleeping, and they placed him up on the shelves' wide lip where it made a small bowl. The seal returned to the water.

Tales of a child running on the Island surfaced some years later. It was said that the place had become strangely haunted, and no craft landed on their shores without the loss of all. As the story grew in the telling, the sea farers began to take a wide berth, although it was out of their way. Isolation settled on the area.

Aragant laid siege to the Western Steppes and his black army marched on Ismeral. He killed all in his way. His eye drooped where a dark scar formed across his cheek and brow. It was rumored he had killed Ariel and her child. However, as insurance he had every baby under two killed up and down the Carmel Coasts. Many tales of his cruelty were passed through the Coasts, but some thought he had not killed the baby as the Prophecy foretold. Life went on for most as talk of hatred surfaced in every city.

Then the gates to the Dark were found and opened by Aragant and his magicians. Soon they plundered Mount Moragan's cavernous halls. The Book of Prophecy lay hidden in the deepest cavern, covered in dust and darkness for over a thousand years.

RETRIEVED

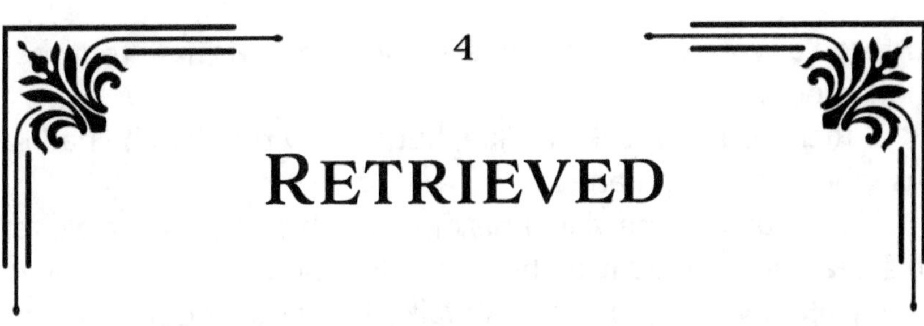

*At the same time, mine understanding returned to me,
and for the glory of my kingdom,
my majesty and brightness returned to me....*
Daniel 4:36

The Silkies looked with sadness at the craft approaching them from the West, as storm clouds thundered out in the distant East Sea. They had not aged or changed during the years they cared for Riel Agam; only their curly hair was longer which had already dried in the sea air. Their son stood between them. Already taller than both Silkies, Riel was lank but physically fit for his twelve years. None of them uttered a word for it was understood that their time together had ended.

Riel tried to speak in Silkie, but Liberty told him he had to use the speech of man.

They placed the vial of his mother's blood on a chain over his head and rested it on his chest. He spoke but they moved away silently, weeping as they walked towards the shore. They were not comprehending in any language as a combination of sadness and joy to be free of human form swept over them. They stopped just at the edge of the waves and with tears flowing they turned to Riel. He went to their arms, and they held him close.

With a choked voice, Liberty said, "Riel we have done our best, but we must leave."

"Remember our teachings, always praise God, and never forget your origins." They kissed his forehead and cheeks before diving into the waves transforming back into seals. Soon they were cavorting, twisting, and turning in the sea. Riel watched them as they both jumped out of the waves each performing a synchronized somersault, their sorrows momentarily forgotten. Then suddenly they were gone. Liam rowed through the froth and currents and landed a few feet from Riel.

"I have come for you," Liam said.

Riel stammered as human speech was still little foreign to him, "Whaaaaaat will happen to my Mothers? And what of the issslands and the others?"

"Your real Mother gave her life to put you on this island Riel. And life will go on here as it has since the beginning. The Silkies will live long past your life span. They are very wise in their own ways and these islands will not be visited by man for many years."

The boy looked full into Liam's face. "May I pray before we leave?"

"Of course," replied Liam. He handed Riel a stack of clothing and a pair of comfortable worn boots and a blue, sea farers shirt that had wide sleeves that tapered down to cuffs that covered his arms completely.

"Liam, I've never had anything that covered my arms, isn't this hot and uncomfortable?"

"Riel, the sleeves cover your birthmark," said Liam. "However, the main reason you are wearing it is because you will not be questioned when we land in Krusche. You must never show that mark to anyone, except when you are given a sign. But beyond that, Riel, you can tell that you come from an island but nothing about Silkies or your history. You must promise me because your life will depend on it."

Riel solemnly gave his promise and held both of Liam's hands while he did so. Then he slowly turned back and faced the Islands. He prayed thankfully from his heart about the many incredible things he had experienced in his short life. He mentioned the sweeping vistas, the intense lightning filled storms, the warm cavern he lived in, the sweet bird's eggs, the driftwood fire that warmed his living quarters. But mostly he talked about the many creatures that kept him, as well as the Silkies whose sacrifice brought tears to his eyes. He knew it was painful for them to maintain human form but they both never complained in all the years they helped him. Then he turned back to Liam.

Liam handed him two belts and a scarf encrusted with small pearls and stones. The weaving was very intricate and colorful and like nothing Riel had ever seen, which was not of any great import since the only cloth he had seen came from the booty of ships sunk long before. The shirt already felt itchy on his skin.

Riel inquired, "Where am I going?"

"You were born to a destiny," said Liam. "The Silkies taught you of the water but now you must walk with men and animals. I will be with you on many occasions in the next years. Know this: The birthmark is the sign of the King Agam. You were given life not by the Silkies but by Adriel, the Queen. She sacrificed everything to have you walk this earth as I told you. It was I who had a few drops of her blood collected in this vial. You are wearing it around your neck. Keep this with you and never remove it as it will restore health and even stop the grim reaper from his prey. Never forget what Adriel sacrificed for you."

"Who then was my father?" Riel asked.

"Ah," said Liam looking tenderly into the boy's face. "He was Aran, Lord of the High Earth. Adriel was his Queen from the Northern Marches. They were betrothed in their youth and were married in the Golden Palace near the Windrift River, high in the Mountains far to the East of here. It was not an easy truce between them as Adriel was high born, determined and utterly stubborn. Their first year was punctuated by much turmoil.

"She resented much of the Palace life until Aran left for three weeks and returned with white roses and the hope of love in his blue eyes. He treated her with such tenderness and compassion that she slowly came to see what a courageous, kind, and loving man he was. She came to love him. Aran was fit for the crown that wore heavily on his head. Put the boots on, please."

"Who am I then?" Riel put the boots on, but they felt foreign and uncomfortable after spending years in open sandals.

"You are Riel Ran Agam, the King Born of the Seas, but for now you will be called Riel or Ran."

They both got into the boat and Liam carefully navigated the surf into the sea. Soon the sun beat down on them and Riel watched the seagulls as they sang goodbye in their squealing high voices above. One even landed on the railing and looked into Riel's face, speaking with slurred squawks, "We didn't know, we didn't know! We thought you were a Silkie and wondered why you were male. What happened? What happened? What are you then? Why are you with Liam? Must we say goodbye? We didn't know! We didn't know!" But before Riel could answer, the seagull took off to communicate with the other seagulls. That is just how seagulls are with their short attention spans.

Soon Riel's eyes began to droop. Yawning, he soon slid down and nestled in the bow of the boat. Liam smiled and covered him over with a tarp from the beating sun.

KRUSHE

*"We wipe the dust of your town from our feet
as a public announcement of your doom."*
Luke 10:11

They landed the next day. The port was bustling with activity as Krushe was a major port on the Carmel Coasts. It was also the end of a major silk route from the inland. High above the city on a steep hill, a pink sandstone castle dominated the skyline for miles.

Below, tidy stone white-washed buildings lined well paved streets. Flower boxes flowed with blooms of every color and variation. The market offered every type of produce or material; silks of every color, vegetables from foreign lands, animals in cages, fresh meats and the finest gold and silver jewelry ever created by men's hands.

Liam and Riel docked just as a huge ship entered the harbor. The masts were taken down from the rigging as the vessel glided into the port, the distance covered in a few short minutes. The docks were a hive of arrival activities.

Riel and Liam docked without notice, just a pair fishing for their supper. Still, Liam had Riel cover his head and ears with a knitted cap as they entered the city. Two finely carved stone Lyons graced the columns at the entrance to the harbor. They were well worn with age and crumbling, few details left on their outlines. Some said they were made during the wars with the South Coast more than a thousand years before. As Liam stepped through the gates, a huge roar escaped from the stone beasts, which was heard even in the castle a half a mile away. Everyone stopped to listen but soon lost interest and resumed their varied tasks.

Riel could not help but stare at the masses of buildings and people. Still, Liam carefully guided him through the gate and onto an avenue leading to the sandstone castle. It zigged and zagged through town, through the marketplace and up the hill. They were halfway through town when Liam stopped to buy several items in the central market. Over the next few hours Liam managed to get a fine-looking black blanket Appaloosa with white spots on his rump, supplies, and a few comforts for the journey they were about to take. Riel watched with awe as camels, horses, people, and children coursed through the market.

He could not get enough of the color and energy of the place. It was hard waiting and watching for Liam as the Lord entered several shops and stalls looking for the necessary items. The sun was setting as the emerged from the market, they changed course to a small side street. They soon came out on the Silk Road.

Liam stopped at the Carson Inn as darkness fell on the town. The Inn was a two-story wood and clay building neatly colored baby blue in contrast to the surrounding buildings. Riel was so tired he followed Liam up a creaky, steep, dark, and narrow set of stairs to a room on the upper floor. He sat on the bed but was in a sort of stupor. Liam kneeled and helped him off with his boots and itchy shirt. He had Riel lay down, but the boy was asleep before his head even hit the pillow.

Liam covered him with a sheet and light blanket and tenderly touched Riel's face.

Liam murmured, "My good boy." He turned down the lamp, left the room, and headed downstairs. He knew the comfort of a bed, sheets and pillow would not be in Riel's future for many months.

The innkeeper looked up just as Liam entered the pub portion of the Inn. Narky was a short stout little man with a largely bald head with two patches of grey bushy hair above his rather large dish shaped ears. His voice, however, was deep and loud reverberating on the pub walls.

Narky said, "I know you. You've stayed here before then?"

"No, I have not stayed here before," said Liam. "A lot of people say I look familiar though. What is on for dinner tonight?"

"My wife cooked a hearty stew with cubed potatoes," remarked Narky.

Soon Liam was sitting with a steaming hot bowl of stew and a pint of ale. Narky kept looking at Liam's face thinking that he knew he had seen him before, but he couldn't recollect where or when. The meal was followed by a bowl of rice pudding, much to Liam's delight.

"Tomorrow Narky, the boy and I will need to leave early," Liam said. "Have you any connections that might want to sell a donkey? We will need him for stamina and to carry our goods."

"I've been trying to sell the stubbornest, stupidest creature you will ever run across," said Narky.

"Everyone here knows his nature and he will do nothing unless enticed by carrots or some of his grain. I've beat him but he will not move unless we feed him. I've nearly lost my shirt feeding the useless thing. You can have him for 20." The currency of the village was EUS. The average worker received 10 EUS a day, or 3,000 EUS a year.

"Prepare him for the journey and be ready before the sun rises. We will need grain and carrots above the supplies we already have then. I understand you make the finest journey cakes in Krushe; can you include a bag of those also? Can you do this and make the boy and I a hearty breakfast besides?"

"For a price we can have that done. What shall we say then? We will have to go out of our way and my wife hates getting up before dawn. A bag of carrots will not be cheap this time of year."

Liam handed Narky two pure gold coins called a Milieus. A Milieus was worth $10,000 EUS. Only the King's treasury held most of these coins and they were rarely seen or used by merchants.

Narky could not believe what he held in his hand. He looked at the coins shining in his palm.

"I don't believe it!" Narky said. "How did you get these coins? I've only ever seen one in the many years I've been a merchant and they far exceed the costs of the things you want in the morning. Why would you overpay me?"

"I must have your absolute silence as to who gave you these," said Liam. "I know your daughter is having problems and about to give birth to her third child. You can use the extra at your discretion."

"I can't load you down with that stupid Donkey then. He will just delay you," said Narky.

"Lawrence the Donkey is just the right animal we need right now, carrots and all. But it very important you get us off before sunrise in the morning with everything we need," said Liam.

The next morning before the stars started to fade, Liam on the horse and Riel riding Lawrence were off down the Silk Road heading inland. The Donkey was particularly compliant as Liam made sure the horse carried all the carrots, with one sticking out of the bag just in front of the Donkey's nose. The Donkey was loaded down with most of the supplies with the boy wedged in a saddle between the bags. Narky, smiling with good fortune, had the coins in his pocket and was rubbing them together as his guests left. It was only after they left, he took one out in the sun to look at the stamped images. He knew the oak leaf and Lyon as the symbol of the kings but fell into wonder at discovering the opposite side held an image of Liam his guest.

It must have been a coincidence. However, the whole town was stirred when two Milieu surfaced in the market a few days later as they also recalled the Lyon's call and so the Prophecy was on the lips of anyone that mattered.

> The Lyons roar at his entry,
> As the return of the Lord compels.
> Two Milieu hold his image,
> as the Prophecy foretells.
> The coins and Lyons are harbingers
> of the beginning of the end.
> For soon the true crown will rise again,
> and darkness will not descend.

Sung in the old language, the words and harmony blended well. The song was forbidden but many of the people remembered it from their lullabies as children. It was often used to comfort and encourage in those days. Now, because of the coins and Lyons, the tune was sung in taverns and pubs across Krushe as the people took hope in the return of the Lord.

But among those listening were Aragant's spies and minions.

Already at the edge of the Krushe, two caravans were preparing to leave having traded their silks and goods. They were returning with salt, hard spun cloth, jewelry, and many other items from the sea trade.

Belial, the towering leader of the caravan with a swarthy complexion and a cold, piercing gaze, observed the Appaloosa file past with a man leading a young boy wedged between supplies on a donkey. Riel felt a shiver go down his spine as his eyes met with the man's pointed stare. The boy sensed real danger and dropped his gaze.

Belial did not miss much being the leader of the largest caravan. Something about the man on the horse bothered him but he could not put his finger on it. He was called away by trouble with some of the camels and a fist fight. It pestered him all morning as the stifling waves of air glittered with the noon heat.

The caravan should have left before dawn but the men working the docks were slow to get the goods transported to the edge of town. He just knew that man's face from somewhere. His crew knew that a deep scowl meant punishment and trouble and having a delayed start meant retribution anyways. They dodged and avoided Belial and he became more and more agitated as the day wore on.

Liam turned and looked at the irritated caravan leader as they topped the last small hill leading out of town. The caravan formed a line at last and started to leave in the opposite direction. Liam turned to Riel.

"Riel, we are going to be recognized soon by the leader of the caravan back there," Liam said. "They are going in the opposite direction because they do not know who we are yet. The milieu will surface, and the Lyons roar will be recalled. But, before then, in the matter of a few hours the worst of the false king's men will turn to pursue us, and his horses come from the desert and are much swifter and will quickly catch up."

Riel felt a chilling shudder go through his body. "Liam, what can we do? Are we trapped?"

Liam smiled at Riel and said, "You must hold on and just trust that where I take you is the best route."

"We have only the horse and this silly Donkey Liam.... We will not get far," said Riel.

"Ah, but Riel, sometimes the most stubborn, cantankerous types can outthink a wily desert warrior, even though he is as sly as a fox," said Liam. Lawrence looked at Liam's face, content to be crunching on a carrot Riel gave him and to be standing still while the discussion continued.

Liam moved in front of Lawrence and appeared to be talking with the animal. The funny braying went on for a few minutes which confused Riel, but he waited to see the outcome. Riel partially understood some of the words, but they did not make sense to him.

Liam put Riel into the saddle on the Appaloosa, grabbed the reins and took off running towards a copse of trees entirely off the road. Liam eventually jumped on the Lawrence's back between the supplies. The Donkey took off at a pace even the horse could hardly keep. The trees were thick, and darkness filled the shadowed depths beneath. Lawrence wound up and down following what appeared to be a giant serpents trail. Liam did not slacken the pace unless Lawrence stopped to sniff the air and see ahead. They continued until late afternoon when they came to a flat, open area filled with miles of wheat, barley, and flax fields. Liam turned and stopped for a minute looking back towards the city which had long faded behind the distant hills.

Riel was content to stop and just watch Liam's face as he stood looking off into the distance. Riel was tempted to asked about the scars but understood Liam was searching the air for something and so waited. Riel decided Liam had an unremarkable face, but he liked it.

The caravan was making its first stop for water when Belial suddenly stopped pacing.

His face darkened in fury as he turned towards his men. He suddenly shouted a series or orders at the top of his powerful voice. His men exploded into action and six men, and six prized and swiftest of the desert horses were brought to the leader. They were a vicious looking group as they mounted their beautiful steeds. All the men had dark eyes, born of the deep desert with their ruthless scorpion hearts. All had numerous scars covering their dark skin as their "practice" battles with their curved swords often produced results that left them marked as warriors. Each of them was a true hunter in the meanest sense of the word, often leaving hurt and bleeding people and animals behind to suffer and die in agony. They knew exactly where to put their blades to exact the greatest pain. All of them were dressed from head to toe in a black turbans and matching robes, under trousers as well as black studded boots with silver spikes. A red scimitar dominated a silver background embroidered on each man's sleeves. Although the heat was oppressive none of them seemed to notice as they had lived in heat far worse for most of their existence. They turned as one back the way they had come.

Bilial cursed himself for allowing valuable quarry a ten-hour lead. He knew that face well; it was etched on the back of coins in the King's treasury. Liam looked younger and more vibrant on the coin, but he was sure it was him. He had been the King a thousand years before the fall of the desert people. It was foretold in many of the Holy Books that one day Liam would return and the false King holding the throne would be annihilated. It had been twelve years since Aragant had murdered Adriel Agam the Queen and what he thought was the last of the royal family and their lineage. Somehow the son had escaped his grasp. He was sure he had removed the child by the killing of hundreds of babies along the Carmel Coast. Belial cursed and swore again for allowing the huge lead. But then, how could a man and a boy allude them for long on these horses?

The prophecy had always haunted him, and now what would Riel's survival mean for him and the King? This mission was not only about bounty; it was about securing his own future.

Liam looked out behind from where they had come and said to Riel, "The pursuit begins. We will get to Uriel just in time."

Liam got off the Donkey and swung up onto the horse, wedging Riel in front of him on the saddle. He kicked the horse and set an incredible pace across the valley filled with wheat and barley fields, gracefully jumping the horse across several low stone fences. Lawrence did his best to keep up but gradually fell some distance behind.

The pursuers were another matter altogether, as they had already crossed the distance to Krushe in a few short hours. One of the riders peeled off from the main group and headed straight for the hilltop Palace, as the others continued through the hills. Two hours later, Belial stopped them as he lost the trail crossing the last of the hills. He carefully backtracked and found a set of tracks heading off towards another copse of trees. He inspected the ground and foliage. He announced to his men, "They are heading towards the Western Steppes across the Wheaton Valley."

Even though his horse sides were heaving in the heat, he remounted and pressed into the forest. Soon he saw more evidence of passage but confusingly it was going back towards the sea. He stopped and followed the trail on foot for about a hundred yards. Then he remounted as his face contorted in consternation. Why would they head for the wilderness and backtrack? His gut told him he had the right trail and the right direction, so he decided to trust it. This scenario recurred four more times until he realized the path was made to slow him and his men to a crawl. It had worked but Belial now knew they had to be going to the Steppes and he headed straight for the Wheaton Valley at top speed.

They arrived to see a marked path through the wheat and barley heading straight across the Valley. He was not often duped but he had wasted valuable time. They flew across the fields careless about the damage they did to the crops by fanning out. The stone walls were nothing to the Desert horses.

Miles away Liam and Riel started winding through a series of low rolling hills.

Carefully Liam worked his way down a stream bed gulley. "Riel, get off the horse and let him go. Carefully place your feet where my feet are going to leave an imprint in the stream bed. You must do this as quickly as possible but make sure they are in my footprints." Riel immediately complied.

Liam struck the horse's rump sending it galloping up the hill and out of sight. Lawrence looked at Liam. "Follow Riel's footprints just I just instructed." Liam sprinted down the stream with Riel following and Lawrence trailing them. Lawrence could easily place his front two hoofs in the footprint, but his back hoofs mostly missed the mark; He was trying hard, his ears were straight back on his head, whimpering and crying as he went.

However, Lawrence was used to complaining. He would slow from time to time trying to get exact placement crying out even worse if he missed.

Liam stopped to laugh at Lawrence. The animal was some distance behind them by this time, so Liam called him and told him to forget the footprints. The Donkey rapidly caught up to them. They were standing in a small cove, their feet in six inches of water with a cliff lip ten feet above them.

He carefully hoisted Riel up to the top of the lip. The boy looked down from above laying on his stomach looking over the edge.

"You see those three trees in the distance Riel?" said Liam. "I want you to wait until you are somewhat dry sitting on the rock next to you. Then break off a branch from the brush next to you, carefully remove your shoes, and walk to the trees trailing the bush behind you and leaving not a single footprint. Be slow and careful not to disturb any vegetation on the way. When you get to those trees, one of them has a large root sticking out of the ground. Go around to the other side of the root and look at the base, you will see a small space opens below the ground. Carefully and slowly wedge your body in that space using the branch and bush to cover any disturbance. Then pull the branch in front of you covering what is left of the opening so you are well hidden. You must wait until I send for you in that small space.

"DO NOT FEAR! It should only be a few hours. You must not make a sound when they stop to inspect the area where you are. Freeze as the Silkies taught you, not making even the sound of your breath. Can you do this Riel?"

Riel got up turned and walked over to the rock to wait while his legs, pants, and feet dried. Then he broke off a branch from the nearby bush. The branch was large, but it fanned out and was easy to trail behind him. He took his time working his way over to the three trees walking backwards most of the way using the brush to obliterate any signs. He crawled below the root but part of the roots roof caved-in revealing a deeper depression where an animal had lived. He was able to wedge himself deeply under the root with his head near the entry. He pulled the branch into the opening, and he was perfectly hidden and even able to look out in front of him. He carefully and rhythmically began to sing a song the Silkies taught him, and his breathing slowed as his imagination made him part of the growing tree, with sap flowing and deep roots below. He was in a trance an hour later and totally comfortable in his hideout beneath the ground.

Liam turned to Lawrence as Riel was drying off above. "Riel has done what I needed him to do as the coming flood water would have carried him away. Now Lawrence you can put on a show if you want. I need you to take the quickest easiest path down this stream making as much disturbance as you want." Liam got onto Lawrence's back. Lawrence took off splashing and running as fast as he could down the stream side where there were fewer rocks. Liam was tossed and almost toppled with the supplies jiggling and flying as they went.

Far to the West a sudden and very violent storm dumped an inordinate amount of water into the stream's headwaters.

An hour later, Belial was inspecting the place where Liam had walked into the stream. He had a particularly nasty look on his face as he twisted his mustache between his fingers. He was very tired and so were his horses. Soon they would have to rest but he knew his quarry was not far ahead.

The problem was the decision to follow the horse as the boy might be on it or continue with Liam's footprints. Soon he realized that Liam's footprints were underneath the donkey's hoof mark. This was very strange indeed, since when did donkeys follow footprints, and the animal was doing a good job of it too? In the West he could see huge thunderclouds building as he looked back. He could hear distant thunder. He slowly worked his way up the stream observing the prints and decided that the boy was also putting his feet where Liam had walked so they both were going downstream. The horse was a ruse to slow him down. His men were extremely nervous as Belial was never a man of silence and he had not uttered a word in the last two hours.

Belial shouted for his men to mount and ride. They entered the water as the sides of the stream gradually steepened ahead. Soon they were in between two ten-foot escarpments where water wore the soft soils away. They were so intent on the chase they did not realize how quickly the water was rising until their horses started struggling. Belial turned and looked back to see a huge wall of water not 200 feet behind them. He screamed and hit the horse just as the other men realized what had happened. They all panicked and beat their mounts to go forward. The sound was deafening behind as the soft soil collapsed along the walls and trees and bushes were uprooted in the flooded stream. The boiling water soon caught them right where Liam had hoisted Riel up. Roiling and shouting the men were soon overcome with their mounts lost and the heavy gear on their bodies weighing them down.

Two bodies and two horses washed up further downstream catching between boulders as the stream widened out into a small valley. Belial sat on the shore half drowned and his horse standing beside him. He sat recovering for a few minutes soaking wet. He had lost his supplies and discarded almost all his weapons to save his life. He was moved beyond anger to a rage that knew no bounds. He decided to backtrack the canyon taking the upper dry trail following what was left of the canyon wall. He was hunting for his men and their horses and any sign of his quarry. He found one of his men, half dead hanging from a tree limb ten feet above the ground.

It took him some minutes as he got the man down and tried to revive him. He put the man up on his horse, but he collapsed forward. Belial saw three trees and one of his horses up ahead. He needed the shade and the time and so he walked his horse to them. He managed to retrieve the other horse and laid his man down on the ground in the shade. The man regained consciousness, coughing, and spitting up water. Another man dragged up the hill to the trees with his horse in tow.

Riel could see the horse standing squarely through the bush, right in front of him. He carefully controlled his breath as he heard two men approach. Slowly, a breath in, a breath out. The two men were arguing but Riel could not make it out until one of them stepped in front of where Riel was hidden. He could see dirt and mud on the spiked boots, and a jeweled blade handle sticking out the top of his footwear.

Belial yelled, "We will pursue them downstream. If I find that boy, I will be sure to torture him with a thousand small cuts with my blade before tying him between our horses to be drawn and quartered."

"We don't have enough horses to do all four limbs, sir. It would be thirds I believe," said his man, still half dazed and prone to exactness.

"What?"

"Thirds, sir. We are half drowned and we need rest and to let our horses recuperate, sir. I have a couple of the mibre cakes left in my pack that did not get soaked. Besides, look at Ribre he is just now starting to breathe normally. We can torture that little son of a gun when we catch him, and we will catch him with you in charge." He was also prone to flattery when given any opportunity.

Belial had realized that Liam must have dumped the boy as he had not seen imprints in the water just as the flood overtook him and his men.

The trees were located on a small hill above the rolling terrain. Belial surveyed the surrounding area. "There is nothing moving, and we will rest here a few minutes to let our clothes dry and eat your cakes. The horses must recover too, or I would make you move on!"

Riel heard every word clearly as he could make out the stitching on Belial's boots as he paced back and forth in front of the root, making a furrow in the soil. It seemed laughable that Belial was less than two feet away making these terrible threats, but the danger was too great and Riel returned to his breathing exercises. Breathe in, he thought, and breathe out... one... two... three... four.

Liam was a few miles away with Lawrence. Liam had crawled up on top of a glacial boulder deposited a millennium before, and he had his hands clasped together behind his back. He was looking back to where Riel was hidden and now trapped with Belial. "Just stay still and use your Silkie chant to not make a sound," he murmured under his breath.

Liam suddenly turned around and said, "It has been many years my friend Uriel!"

A huge grizzly bear suddenly erupted out of the pine trees grumbling and growling.

"I will have you know I was having a nice nap in the afternoon sun," Uriel answered.

Indeed, there was dried berry juice and a long-forgotten fish remnant in his coat below his mouth. He was very rumpled and had a bigger hump than usual from sleeping with his paws facing up lying beside a rock in soft meadow grass. He was very out of sorts.

Liam gave him a look that froze him in his tracks.

"OK. Okay!! Sorry, Liam."

The Filk Bear was 11 feet tall when standing. His bulk disguised an agile body of well-toned muscles. Despite his crabby and disheveled appearance, he was a great warrior and had the years and the scars to prove it. He could run 35 miles an hour in short spurts, lope for many miles and not sleep for many days. One of the last of his line in this part of the world, Aragant had hunted his kin to the brink of extinction. Lawrence looked at the bear with disdain. He, at least, did not let drippings dry on his chin.

"Uriel, I need you to take Riel to the Isles of Paradise," remarked Liam.

"That is more than one thousand miles from here and who is Riel that a Filk Bear would accompany a human through that terrain? It is a wild and dangerous journey. I won't do it," said Uriel. "I'm getting older now and besides, how will I eat along the way? This place has a nice berry patch."

"I can see that Uriel," said Liam. "It is evident in your appearance. Riel will be free shortly and you must go back with Lawrence and retrieve him and protect him and the Donkey until you get to the Isles."

"I eat Mules," remarked Uriel.

Lawrence heard that remark and turned towards the bear. He let out a loud bray which caused Uriel to jump. Uriel was not expecting a reaction from the Donkey. He suppressed his startled jump, but it was too late, and it started a chain reaction in the loose shale he was standing on. Liam and Lawrence were standing on the boulder watching as Uriel used every bit of finely tuned reactions to stay upright as the hillside, slowly cascaded down the mountainside. When he stopped falling, he was left sneezing and covered in a fine layer of grey dust at the bottom.

Liam chuckled and Lawrence brayed. Lawrence was very pleased with this result as he had been deeply insulted that Uriel had called him a Mule.

Liam said to Uriel, "You are going now, and you will follow the D-O-N-K-E-Y. You will wind through the great wasteland, across the White Lake, and on to the Salton Sea. Then you will cross the mountains using Rippon's Pass and go on to the Gate. You WILL leave right now, and you will not engage Belial."

"BELIAL!" Uriel screamed. "I will rip him to pieces. He killed my mate and my last two cubs. I will track and rip him to pieces for what he has done to my family!" At this point the bear started shaking. That evolved into an effort to remove the dust. The rotation began at his hindquarters and then worked his way up to his face, his whole body rotating in a half circle back and forth until he stopped. A huge cloud of dust surrounded the bear, and he was sneezing and coughing again.

"NO," said Liam. "You will do exactly as I have told you. I am handing over the child of the Prophecy to you. Riel Ran Agam the son of King is here and in your charge."

Uriel shimmied again, and another huge cloud of dust surrounded the bear, and he was sneezing and coughing for a third round.

Then the bear stood still for a moment, "Now wait, what child of the Prophecy? I am not equipped to handle a little kid. They eat like three times a day. I will return to my cave and think about this. I am rather hungry and Filk bears do not traffic with donkeys on any basis. Look at the worn pads on my paws. Do you think 1000 miles is going to do anything for them?"

Liam now used a loud voice and said, "Uriel. URIEL you will follow Lawrence back and retrieve Riel. Those pads have a lot more than 1000 miles in them. You stop this delay and follow my instructions to the letter. Understand? I want you to promise me."

Uriel thought for a moment then solemnly promised. Bears know better than to cross Liam.

The bear started mumbling under his breath as soon as he turned to follow Lawrence back to Riel. He turned to say goodbye, but Liam was nowhere to be seen.

6

RECUPERATION

"Let the redeemed of Jehovah say so,
Whom he hath redeemed from the hand of the adversary."
Psalms 107:2

Riel had crawled out from below the root an hour after the men and their horses left. What he saw made him very leery, for behind Lawrence a huge, growling grizzly bear was approaching. It took courage to stand there and wait but he knew Liam had a plan, so he waited.

The bear smelled Riel from some distance away as a slight wind carried his scent, and the scent of Belial and his horses and men. Uriel started thinking about Belial and his hackles went up on his back, he started growling and a vicious look was on his furry face. He knew if he could just break away, he could track Belial as the scent was fresh and easy to follow. However,

Filk bears never go back on their word and he had promised Liam to take on Riel.

Riel was further repelled by the look and rancid smell of the bear. It was unbearable when Uriel walked right up and sniffed Riel from head to toe. Riel started retching as the ripe fish stuck in the bear's fur suddenly dislodged.

Lawrence said, "My God bear when was the last time you did anything to clean yourself? Look what you have done. The poor kid is repulsed by your smell." Uriel was very surprised that he also could use human speech. Riel looked at Lawrence with new respect.

A portion of the cliff had collapsed, and the stream was now easily accessible. Uriel turned and went down and got right mid-stream and took a bath. He sat out there some length of time as Lawrence and Riel built a small hidden fire near the root where Riel had been concealed. Riel made hot tea and cooked a pan of spicy beans from the pack on Lawrence's back. Riel gave Lawrence a few carrots and brushed down his coat. It was nice not to be running and Uriel had returned to camp still wet. He collapsed in a heap near the fire.

They all rested for an hour, but Uriel felt uneasy as the scents in the air told that Belial and his men were still nearby. Uriel prompted them to pack up and head towards the pass. It didn't take long for them to get going but Riel was having trouble staying awake, so Lawrence had him climb up on the saddle. They made better progress but stopped at midnight near a rocky crag. Riel was in a stupor as he laid out his sleeping bag and crawled in. The moonlight shone on snowy jagged mountains lining the distant skyline.

Over the next six weeks the three of them made steady progress towards the mountains. The days passed in monotony as Uriel set a grueling pace with little time for food, or even a break. But he made sure no one would pick up even a hint of their trail. He often went behind checking and obliterating any sign as Lawrence and Riel headed for a landmark he had pointed out.

7

PALACE OF THIEVES

"God is not a man, that he should lie,
Neither the son of man, that he should repent:
Hath he said, and will he not do it?"
Numbers 23:19

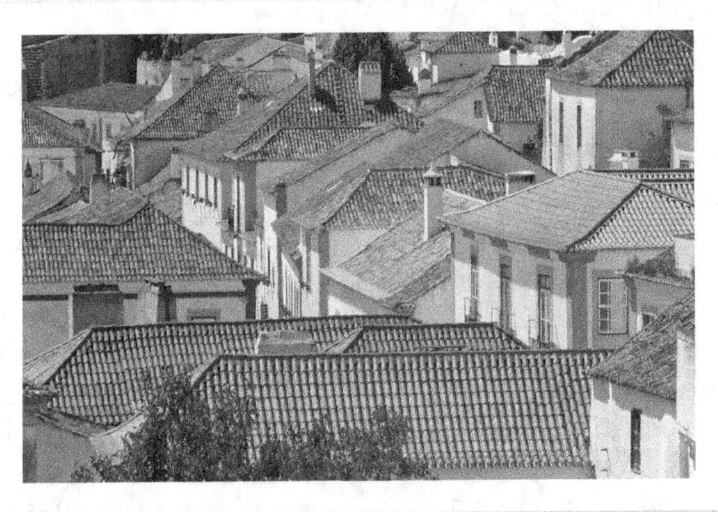

Six weeks later, Belial stood mid-room, and he pushed the point of his blade deep into the ornate carved, rosewood table in front of him. The room was hung with bright tapestries from centuries before and even having faded they still told of life: hunting scenes, kings and queens long buried but the main theme seemed to be beautiful, elegant women in their long, jeweled dresses. The afternoon light came in across the table shedding a band of brightness which reflected onto the clouds and blue skies painted on the ceiling. A huge fireplace dominated the room and even now kept the room warm. Lyons were carved around the mantle and their eyes were set with precious stones. The effect was ostentatious but very comfortable.

The King entered his mouth twisted in rage. "You call yourself a Desert Fox? Yet a young boy and Donkey escape your grasp, your men, horses, and supplies lost in a flood, and then you can't even track them. I should have had my Jester follow them; he would have done a better job."

Belial walked right up to the King, bent slightly, and put his face six inches from the King's face. He coolly replied, "I doubt if anyone could have stood up to Liam and his interference. I lost men I personally trained, and we have been together thirty-years!" He walked back to the table and plunged the knife deep into the ornate surface.

"No need to destroy my furniture, Belial," the King answered. "Then it is as we feared, and the rumors are true coming out of the Carson Coasts: The Lyons have spoken at the Gates; the Milieu have surfaced, and you have seen Liam yourself. The Prophecy begins. I would have expected you to have done your job when you saw the two of them leaving Kruche instead of ignoring them."

Belial said, "I would have killed them if I had known who they were. As it was, I was told the child was killed twelve years ago when Aragant murdered the Queen. Who was it exactly that fostered that lie? It was only because I saw drawings and paintings in the Holy Book years ago, and his image on the coins, that I eventually recognized Liam. Liam must have had a part in hiding the heir or the boy would never have escaped Aragant. But that is not my fault, is it? At least now you know it has started and we can stop it."

At this point a scruffy old man, Aristate, shuffled in wearing an old, rather scratchy and worn robe. He interrupted them.

"I have come my King," said the man bowing deeply. "Have you the crystal and the woman?" inquired the King.

At this a small, very beautiful woman entered the room. Her appearance changed, however, as drool began to leak from her mouth as her eyes darted warily around the room.

Le Moya was very thin and although not more than 20, known throughout the land for her precognition skills. Her long blonde hair was wound into a tight braid wound with gold chains and pearls which cascaded down her slender back.

The old man cleared a small table and put a soft white cloth across it. Then he drew out a tripod of pure gold from his robe and put a large irregular crystal in the mount. The woman took a seat and stared deeply into the gem in front of her. Suddenly a swirling-colored light formed inside the shining clear quartz. It had a ghastly effect on the girl, as her eyes crossed, and she began to foam at the mouth. He limbs began to twitch and shiver but her face remained immobile an inch from the surface.

Outside the clouds gathered as an afternoon storm swept across the gulf into the Capital. The tower where the group met began to emanate light and a huge thunderhead formed above it. Where a moment before the flags stood still and unfurled in the afternoon sun, now they whipped and cracked in a blinding rain. A lightning strike hit the window where, only a moment before, the King and Belial had stood looking out.

The woman was now shaking form head to foot, but her face remained static in front of the crystal. Suddenly she stood up and then collapsed into Aristate's waiting arms. He held her gently as they whispered to each other. He softly wiped her now blood-stained mouth and removed the foam off her face and cheeks. She was carried out of the room on a stretcher by the guards.

The King could not wait. "What is it Aristate? What did your daughter see in the stone?"

"Liam has indeed returned," said Aristate. "The boy is of the Prophecy and is already near the shores of the White Lake. Where he is going and what he is doing is not revealed but he is heading north and east. He is accompanied by a Filk bear and a donkey. They are traveling quickly but will soon enter the Galilean Shores crossing the Salton Sea. You will have to send the Dragon if you want to catch them." Belial shivered at this suggestion. "My daughter cannot read the gem for another thirty days as each use takes a little of her life force and she is depleted finding this out for you." Aristate was concerned for his daughter as he had never seen her remain for so long a time in the crystal's grasp.

The King said, "I wonder should I waken the Dark one? The Dragon? He is still bound but I could have him released."

The old man stood a moment clutching his lengthy ragged, grey beard, and then he started pacing the floor. "If we waken the Dark one, there is a chance he may turn on us all and destroy the very thing we are working to preserve, your throne and our power to rule. If we do not wake him, the boy may prevail and fulfill the return of his Kingdom and rule. No, I do not think it is time to waken such evil, but I would alert the temple and the Nuns of Darkness. They may be able to delay the boy and help us destroy him without the Dragon."

"Leave us," shouted the King. This startled Aristate. He looked wide-eyed for a moment and then, in one fluid movement gathered the crystal, tripod and cloth and shoved it all in his robe. He was out of the room before the King could turn to Belial.

"It is I who will be the instrument to take this boy's life!" said the King. "I will attend to the Nuns and have them attend the black Dragon immediately. He may be persuaded to fly Aragant to his men in the wilderness if we give him a crown jewel and twenty horses to eat. He has not had a feast like that in many years and his chains must be wearing on him." The King rubbed his hands together in glee at the thought. He turned and headed to the door, yelling at the posted guards as he passed them. He headed down the stairwell from the tower.

Aragant met King Char La Tan in the narrow stairwell. The King was pale and strangely drained from the meeting and his decision to release the Dragon.

"I just saw the Sorcerer Aristate, he told me what his daughter saw," Aragant remarked. "What do you intend to do and how will we defeat this boy? What of the Dragon my liege?"

"The boy has achieved the White Lake and two Milieus have surfaced in Kruche," said the King. "The Prophecy begins, and some believe I am doomed. But we will defeat them all! My wives and concubines no longer please me and I have heard whispers of dissension from them.

Kill all of them tonight except for Salome and my first wife. Leave my children however."

"Did not my cousin Isabella please you?" Aragant asked. "You have only seen her once my liege."

"You may let her live but send her back to your family along with that other young girl she likes, ah I don't remember her name," said the King.

"Sophia," muttered Aragant in disgust. The child was only ten years old, but the King had her anyway.

Aragant continued, "We are not through or defeated by any means. Think about it: There is nothing but a 12-year-old boy, a Filk bear, and a Donkey standing between us and ultimate power. Liam cannot see the unkindness of men and seeks only their welfare. We will rule and dominate for a thousand years. You need only give me the order and I will ride and release the Black Dragon again."

"Yes, release that malicious thing," replied the King. "Last time we let him go he ate my wife who had gotten fat anyway. But he also ate my favorite daughter and I miss her to this day. I did not know she took my little girl with her when I told her to go rest in my country estate." The King had a tear in the corner of his eye.

Aragant was snickering about the wife. Neat trick sending her to the country estate knowing the Dragon was about to be released the next day. It was Aragant who freed the beast and left a carcass trail to the summer castle. The Dragon being as appreciative as Dragons get. He allowed Aragant to live because he released him, but the Dragon ate all the guards and horses as well as the carcasses neatly left for his consumption on his way to the Summer Castle.

It was a good day as the guards were hand chosen for their lack of "commitment" to the King. One even had commented he thought the king was a pervert for forcing a ten-year-old child. So, all in all a win. However, it was two years before they could capture the beast. and the thing had done much damage.

Aragant said, "What is that mere boy, bear and donkey to our armies?"

Still the King looked dire until he remembered they had captured a princess from the enemies to the north. She was reputed to be a resistant fireball. Even now, she would be bathed, dressed in layers of silk, and left in the bedroom tower for his delight. He licked his lips. "Do not take the life of my new concubine either Aragant." He descended the stairwell quickly.

Aragant relished the thought of controlling the most vicious, powerful, and dangerous thing on the planet. Only he had the name of the beast, and he destroyed every known record after he learned what the true name meant. Years before, he just happened to grab an old scroll while at the temple and didn't even realize what he had. He put the pieces together when he was serving in the Northern Reaches: He stopped to talk with an elderly priest in the remote temple and told him about the scroll he had read and how confusing the text was. The priest explained what the words meant in the old language and then informed the last words were a name, not a place as Aragant had supposed. When the Dragon lair was found and the beast captured two years later, Aragant figured out more about the Dragon. Then after that, Aragant remembered the words from the scroll, which read, "Shadow the beast, ride him at will, keep him below, his will in your tow, but do not look him in his swirling eye."

Aragant realized even with Dragon's true controlling name, if he ever looked him in the eye the reptile would be released from bondage. A sobering and awful thought: He had seen some of the carnage the animal had left behind and some of the men who had suffered from incinerations or the thing's rapier claws. He shuddered but still the thought of flying again, now that was worth every dangerous bit.

CROSSINGS

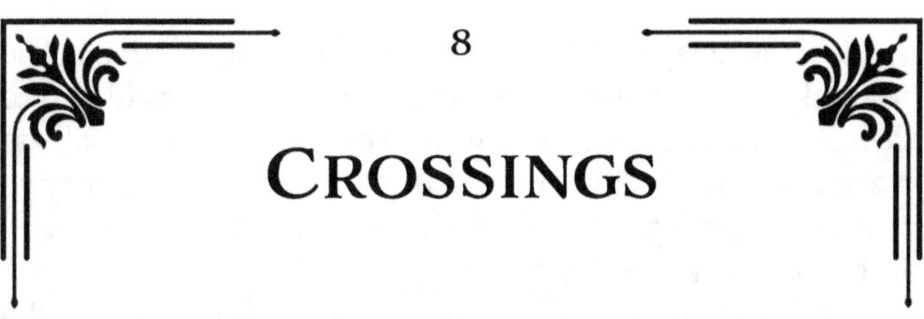

*"And he entered into a boat,
and crossed over and came to his own city."*
Matthew 9:1

The sunset was stunning with its auburn bands across the horizon. Storm clouds were breaking apart and the boat was rocking gently against the pier. Uriel stood hesitating. His weak eyes and powerful sense of smell told him he was going places even he did not imagine. A boat was the last thing a bear wanted to enter. However, true to his promise, Uriel took a tentative step into the boat as the was not sure the craft would hold his mighty bulk. He committed and deftly got in for a bear. Lawrence watched, terror gripping him.

Riel laid out four small carrots down the dock and put one inside the boat. Lawrence would not move. Riel walked up to Lawrence and looked into his wide brown eyes. The animal was shaking. Even if the bear did manage to find the boat, after so many years sitting un-used inside a shed, it was he who was putting his life on the line.

Uriel turned his head as far as it would go to look at the mule-donkey thing. He daren't move anything else sitting in the boat's middle beneath the tied sail. He started laughing and said, "So Mule, are you the brave animal you would have us to believe you are? I could tell you were a coward from the moment I met you."

At this, Lawrence walked across the dock, stood next to the boat, shaking still, proceeded to put his front hoofs in the boat. Now he was half in and out. Riel had to guide his rear end correctly into the craft, but it started rocking with the new weight being uneven. Riel grabbed his reigns and got in front of the terrified Donkey.

"Listen to me Lawrence," said Riel with his most comforting and peaceful voice. "I need you to slowly, slowly lay down but keep your weight in the center of the boat." It was too late, Lawrence fainted dead away when a small wave started the boat rocking again. Fortunately, he did land with his weight centered, only because Riel shoved him as he fell. "Uriel, you have to lay down completely too." The bear not wanting to watch anyway, closed his eyes and laid completely flat in the boat.

Riel soon had them free and untied, off with the wind catching the sail. So good to be on water again. Such a pleasant feeling to skim across the waves, thought Riel as he set his course across. Riel sat at the tiller, the thrill of sailing lifting his heart.

It had been a long haul across the wasteland. Uriel had complained incessantly about his sore pads and Lawrence and Uriel were often at odds with each other, causing the bear to stomp off and leave them behind. Riel usually had a good sense of the direction to follow and just kept going. Sometimes Lawrence would purposely set a good pace and leave the bear behind in his dust. One morning, Riel decided to have a good look at Uriel's paws and the bear obediently held them so he could look at them. He was surprised to see how huge they were as they were bigger than Riel's face and lined with five huge nasty looking claws.

Riel felt in between the pads and was surprised to find a few fine bone fragments shaped like needles sticking into his skin. They were stuck in the fur and the bear could not remove them. Riel yanked a few of them free but two on his back paws remained solidly stuck. The bear yelped every time one was taken out. Lawrence came close to observe the operations.

"Lawrence," said Riel, "do you think you could yank on these needle things with your teeth if I helped you?" Lawrence made a face, and it was so funny that Riel burst out laughing.

"EWHHHHHH!" Lawrence spit on the ground and walked off in a huff.

Riel grabbed the first needle bone in his teeth, got the fur out of the pad, and gave a yank. It came free. He then pulled out the second needle bone. Riel had never tasted anything so vile. He rinsed out his mouth several times in a nearby stream, but it left a filmy, sickening taste that gradually went away two days later. He made the bear stay and went and got ointment out of his supply bag.

"You know Uriel, had you told me earlier about your pain, I would have done this for you."

"I told you every single day since we left," replied Uriel, now laying out in a position of utter relief.

"That's not true. You only said they hurt, not that you had bone like needles in your pads. I know you bears are all proud but instead of complaining why didn't you simply ask for help?"

"Because I'd rather deal with the pain than have the embarrassment of having someone else take care of my problems," said Uriel. "But now that I feel the relief, it might have been slightly foolish to walk this far. You know I hate that Mule too and I don't want him thinking I'm weak in anyway."

"He is Donkey, not a Mule," said Riel. "I keep telling you to stop bickering with him and now I am asking you to please, give me your word, that you will stop badgering him. I've helped you here now help me out. It is most unpleasant listening to you two all day."

"Well, I will try but it is not me who needs to make a promise, it is him. I promise, okay!" They made much better time forward after that, although Uriel was touchy about the word paw or pads.

Riel shook his head from the memory. Very glad all of that was finished and the wind picked up again and the boat quickly glided across the Lake in less than three hours.

On the other side, Uriel sniffed the air and turned to Riel. "You must be extremely careful to follow my path across Matidran's Marsh. Before the shrinking of the sea, Matridan the Mountain King lay siege on the Lake people's enclave. There are remnants of their town on the other side of the marsh. The Lake people rather than submit, destroyed a natural dam which held back the Salton Sea. It destroyed their town, made the marshes and The King and his troops were never heard of or seen again. They are said to walk the Marsh never resting. That was over five hundred years ago. Gradually the White Lake was refilled with fresh water, the marshes formed, and the Salton Sea grew larger. You and Donkey must not speak or make any sound as you walk. If you must say something whisper it low against my ear. We must move quickly and you, Mule, must keep up."

Uriel did not hesitate and took off at a grueling pace pushing the packed Donkey with the boy to their limits.

The bear kept the pace all afternoon and by early evening they had crossed the Marshland without incident. They stood on the shore of the Salton Sea looking at the few remaining derelict houses of the Lake People.

"Ok, that is finished, but we cannot risk crossing the Salton Sea this late and we are all tired. I think we need to find shelter and fast. It will be a moonless night and we are still on the Marshland fringe.... I would not stay here but I can see you both look exhausted," said Uriel.

"Morning is fine with me," stated Lawrence. "Better than beasts who try to kill a healthy donkey in one marsh crossing. I am glad Liam taught me how to keep in the tracks or I never would have been able to follow the stupid bear so quickly since he kept getting out of sight in front of us."

Uriel ignored the slur and started looking for shelter. Soon they were in the remnants of a house that had all four walls, roof, and a door. They all fell asleep after eating a warm meal.

Before dawn Riel was up searching for a boat. "They must have left a boat somewhere here Uriel." Lawrence was still curled into a ball on the ground as his legs were tired from the long haul the day before and he was snoring loudly.

"So much for not making any noise Riel," said Uriel. "I'm just glad we are through those creepy, smelly Marshlands. I hate that place. But I noticed you really depend on your weakness, Riel. You need to stop thinking your sight is greater than my sense of smell."

"Follow me after I stretch out." Uriel extended out his body and let out a huge yawn and then put his nose up and sniffed the air with purpose. "Boats have a certain scent about them from the men and fish. Even now I sense one, but it might take a few minutes for me to get direction with these breezes. I must concentrate. On second thought why don't you make breakfast, and I will find a boat and come back?"

Uriel went to the beach, he turned and walked out on a small strand of sand sniffing the air. Unfortunately, the water level was too high for him to negotiate the water around the point as he could just make out a small shoreline and a cave behind it. He went back and joined the others.

As soon as he arrived, he explained to Riel the problem. Uriel said, "The cliff face I would need to cross over is too soft to hold my weight and the only other way is to swim. It's rough with the wind out there. I can smell men and they have dressed many fish along that shore. I know there is a boat out there in the cave."

"It's okay Uriel, I have climbed many cliffs and I can get over to the cave. We cannot wait as I am sensing something is going to happen soon," replied Riel. He cleaned up the camp, loaded Lawrence and headed for the cliff. He deftly crawled over the cliff face, working his way around the edge and went to the cave. Sure enough, three boats were stored there with oars and sails. He picked the smallest, the only one he could move down to the shore. Thirty minutes later he was waving happily at Uriel from the water. He soon had it landed and packed for the voyage.

Lawrence walked up to the shoreline. "Oh God, it's my lucky day, the wolf has helped you find another boat for me to go sailing in!"

Riel laughed at Lawrence's use of wolf and his tone and inflection.

Uriel took offense, and said, "It my strength and keen sense of smell guiding you so far, Mule."

"Well look at you with your needle bone-encrusted, puffy footpads and your filthy fur, even Riel has to tell you clean up," said Lawrence.

This really riled up the bear and he began to slowly rock back and forth eyeing Lawrence. "I see no excuse for you coming along with your ungainly hoofs and inability to move quickly. I could easily carry the supplies and you can turn around and head for home but you're not going to get a single carrot along the way."

Uriel smiled, and it scared even Riel.

Wisely placing himself the other side of Riel, Lawrence bowed his front legs and started rocking back and forth and smiling emulating the bear.

Uriel raised up on his hind legs towering over Riel. Riel looked up and said, "Man, Uriel, you are very tall. Has this helped conserve your puffy paws?" He started laughing and after a minute even Uriel had to chuckle.

Uriel sheepishly got down having felt some guilt for letting Lawrence get to him and said, "ONE day, Riel, that damned Mule is going to push me way too far!"

Just then a swallow swooped between the threesome. The bird was chattering incoherently landing on Uriel's head right between his ears. The irritated litany continued while the bear crossed his eyes trying to look upward trying to discover the source of the noise. The bird starting flitting from one of the bear's ears to the other and the flew over to Lawrence. Suddenly, a look of understanding crossed Uriel's face.

"Quickly we need to hide the boat between those two dunes right there. Quickly, there is no time to explain but hurry as fast as you can!" said Uriel. He looked terrified.

Riel and Lawrence had never seen Uriel look frightened and they both leaped into action. Lawrence grabbed the tow rope in his mouth tugging from the front while Riel and Uriel pushed from the rear. The boat was soon between the dunes and Riel put the sail, which was not attached yet, over the whole structure just as hundreds of swallows dived and flew overhead, each carrying a small mouthful of sand. Soon the boat was covered and well hidden. And Riel and Uriel smoothed out the sand, so it looked like a dune. It was a hurried job as they all three ran for the nearest standing structure.

They entered the building and heard something moving below an old wooden box in the corner. Riel moved the box and jumped back as large rat like thing with a squished face, stood up talking to herself and looking very irritated at Riel. "Just plain Stupid. Idiots! Look at that bear's beady eyes. Liam is not going to like this, and I am the one who must help them! If they had not been arguing out on the beach, they could have hidden themselves, but oh no! Here is tiny Mini providing them with bottles and milk. Is it I who must lead them to your gates?" Uriel had flattened himself on the floor trying to see the tiny animal.

Unfortunately, his pads were right in front of the Mini's nose and when she sniffed, she almost fell over backwards.

"My GOD bear, is this what the argument out there was about? They stink worse than anything I have ever smelled, and I am related to a rat you know."

Just then a blood curling sound filled the air and a thud sounded out towards the beach.

"Right now, hurry, hurry! Move that old rug, find the trap door, get yourselves down the ladder and for the sake of your lives be quiet," exclaimed Mini in a terrified voice. "HURRY! HURRY!"

Uriel, Lawrence, and Riel all moved the rug as it was covered in mud and a thick coat of dust from the holes in the ceiling. They rolled it up over the trap door and put it to the side. Then they went down the rickety stairs. Just a moment later a dark shadow went over the building. Uriel, the last to go down, stopped and carefully unrolled the rug putting it back somewhat into position over the trap door. He nodded to Mini and Mini unrolled the rest of the rug after the trap door shut. A huge puff of sand came through the front window which, was long relieved of glass just as Mini shoved with all her might and the rug rolled exactly back into place. The dust was stifling but she quickly wiped remains of a few footprints and threw up more dirt in the air for good measure. She managed the box in the corner just as a huge beast's deep breathing was heard at the door.

Suddenly the door simply shattered into thousands of small pieces. The Dragon roared, ripped open the side of the house and stuck his head into the room. The upright scales on his forehead were enormous, two eyebrows were folded scales on either side of snake like, whirling eyes. The sheer number of needle-like teeth which protruded irregularly from his mouth were overshadowed by two long thick incisors. There were bits of bone, cloth, sinew, and flesh wedged between the incisors and front teeth. His blazing eyes were rotating in in unison a multitude of colors with small black slits in the centers.

"I smell you marmot, come out and give me tasty pre-lunch tid-bit!" The Dragon smiled at the thought and sneezed from all the dust. This collapsed the back wall.

"I see you Dragon, but ha-ha you certainly can't see me, even with your eagle vision. I know your eyesight is much worse in the places of men. Speaking of men, you must be the first of your kind to be a pack Dragon with a man in command of you." Mini darted into a hole in the wall because she knew what was coming.

"It must be you again Mini, no other rat would speak to a Dragon without fear. I smell your fear in this building!"

"Fear of what, an exalted pack animal? You got yourself tied to a man's wishes and now you give two legs a ride across the White Lake and Marshes. Perhaps I could get a few birds to guide you if don't know where the man commands you to go?" Mini knew this was too much for a Dragon to withstand and Mini promptly backed up into her hidden hole.

"It will take a lot more than a Marmot to rouse my anger, oh tasty morsel." At the same time, the Dragon's scales had red tinged tips, his tail was swishing the air in front of the house and Aragant was dancing around trying to avoid being killed, while the serpent's eyes were rotating in a distinctly purple range.

"What is weightier than a scale can measure? A dragon butt! Get it scale?? Butt! Ha ha ha…" Mini tried to laugh with conviction.

"Very funny my morsel. However, you are nothing and I am feeling hungry. Have you seen a human, bear, or donkey anywhere?"

Mini, looking only at the further wall knew better than to ever look in a Dragon's eyes, acted like she had caught his gaze. In a slow voice she said, "Yes, I did… I did… I did… They were heading through the Mountains across the Salton Sea. Uriel was having trouble keeping up because of his tender paws, and Lawrence was doing well. They were enjoying the scenery. Your eyes are so beautiful in that purple color."

The Dragon drew in a gigantic breath and in one mighty puff ignited the whole building thinking he would like a taste of well-cooked Marmot. While the flames were engulfing the building the Dragon searched since fire was with him since birth. He knocked all the room's things around but found nothing.

Oh, the thought of him returning to Aragant to report. He got even more irritated. To think that a marmot made fun of him a stupendous, incredible, mighty Dragon, and poor fun at that.

While the Dragon was inhaling, Mini deftly exited through a hole in the foundation.

She dropped into the basement through a similar hole.

She whispered in Riel's ear, "Are you all okay?"

"Yes," replied Riel whispering as he clamped the Lawrence's mouth shut. Moving to Lawrence's ear he said, "you will thank me later Lawrence, your voice carries very well."

"You must not make a sound, but I will wait with you. Dragons are not known for their patience, and I have irritated the beast into a frenzy so he will not remain on the ground long," whispered Mini.

A few minutes later, the sound of huge wings lifting off was heard as well as a man yelling obscenities. All four waited over two hours before the flames were out and the cellar safe to exit.

Mini checked and the coast was, literally, clear. All four hightailed it to a cliff where they found a cave just big enough to fit them all except the smell of bear got a little intense as the minutes wore on.

Riel asked, "What was that beast thing?" Riel looked at Lawrence who again was too shaken to speak and quivering still. Uriel was busy trying to put out a smoking patch in his fur where a cinder had ignited it. The smell was beyond noxious. "Whew, Uriel, will you please stand by the entrance when you are doing that and try to get the smoke to go outside the cave. I feel sick from the smell."

"You know," replied Uriel, "YOU could take some initiative and help me here."

"I can't. The smell of you is beyond what any human can stand." Riel's lips curled into a smile as he noted the cinder was out and Uriel was fine. Uriel, however, not exactly happy, walked out of the cave and right into the water. He soon turned around and went back to the cave as the water was cold.

"It was that Black Dragon, I know it, Riel. No one else loves to burn things to the ground like he does. I hate that foul thing. Aragant must have discovered his true name and is able to command him," said Uriel as he entered the cave. The smell was better but wet bear fur still has a unique quality.

Mini sat in the center of the three of them and she looked up into their faces. "You were so lucky the swallows saw the Dragon approaching from way off. They sent a messenger to me, and I alerted the cliff swallows and had them ready to cover the boat and signal you about the danger. Liam came through over a week ago and said you would need me and so I waited here for you. You sure make a lot of noise for travelers in this most dangerous place. And you Uriel, my God, I could smell you coming yesterday, don't bears maintain some form of cleanliness? You still reek and now, Liam help us, you are wet." She held her nose closed with her tiny paw. "And really, what is all this about puffy pads, needles, and tender feet? I thought you were second in the world for being fierce!"

Uriel replied, "AND, WHO pray tell is first?"

Just then Lawrence realized they were talking about a live and a real dragon. "DRRRRRR......Agon? Dragons eat mules, horses, and me!" He started to shake uncontrollably and a second later lost consciousness, collapsing right in the middle of them. It was a close shave for Mini, who leaped out of the way at the last second.

"Oh good, now we will have peace and quiet for a few minutes," exclaimed Uriel.

Riel looked at Lawrence. "Man, that Donkey saves himself from a lot of discomfort as he seems to collapse easily. I think it might be best if we all rest until sunset when we can get the boat from under the sand. It is going to take some work to get it back into the water, but we can all work together again if you and Lawrence would stop this continued bickering." He gave a serious look to Uriel. Turning to Mini, he said, "Man, that was clever telling the Dragon we were so far ahead. But I think he will not take long to see we are not on the other side of the Sea and will backtrack. Liam warned me about Aragant and how smart he is and between them they will find us if we do not get going tonight. I know the Dragon can see long distances and why I think not moving in daylight is the wisest course."

"It is not hard to fool a hot-headed Dragon, but I warn you NEVER look directly into that horrible beast eyes," said Mini. "Riel, pay attention: You were almost captured and if I had not scouted the ruins and found that hidden trap door and basement, you would be flambee, toast, recreational-cooked Dragon fodder. Not only that but Lawrence and Uriel would have also been dead. If I had not enflamed tee hee, him and covered your tracks, Lawrence would be resting comfortably but dead in a Dragon's belly. You have got to be quieter, pay more attention and plan better. Who thanks a little marmot though?"

"I do," said Riel. Riel picked up Mini and held her in front of his face. "Thank you tiny warrior and savior of me and my friends. You blessed tiny creature; it is because of you we can do what Liam has set before us."

Mini started to get teary eyed but wiped her face as Riel set her back on the ground. Just then, Lawrence adjusted his body on the ground and let out a snore that surprised all three of them. They all jumped after the encounter they just had.

"Look at what we have to put up with!" Turning to Mini, Uriel said, "Has Liam sent you with us Mini?"

"Of course. Liam knows if anyone is N-O-T capable of getting past a Dragon it is you, the fainting Donkey, and a human who gets involved in bickering. You all need help and Liam sent in the best." Mini preened her fur for a moment and brushed her face.

THE PASS

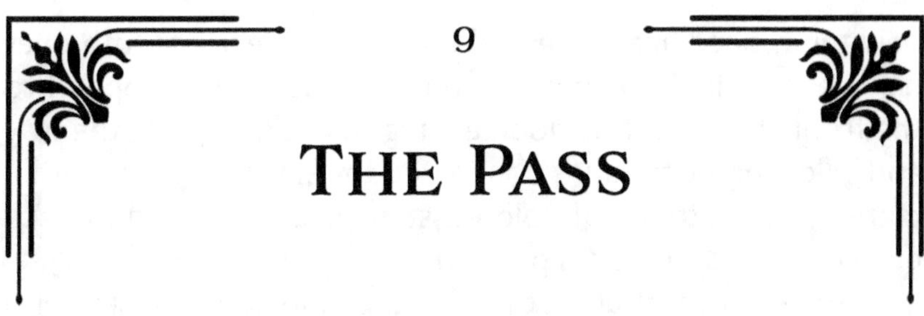

*"Behold, the former things are come to pass, and new things
do I declare; before they spring forth I tell you of them."*
Isaiah 42:9

Later that evening, they all emerged from the cave
refreshed after a hearty meal and rest. They began
work on getting the boat out from under the sand. It
was tough going until Mini enlisted cliff swallows. Their tiny
beaks could do little alone, but working together, soon made
the pile disappear. After the birds finished, the group unfurled
the sail and dragged the craft into the water. Lawrence got in
first, followed by Uriel and Mini.

Uriel was sitting in the bow as the wind caught the sail.
Lawrence had partially recovered but was very nervous about

being in a boat again. He had Mini put a piece of cloth over his eyes and laid down in the boat's middle. Mini hopped to the front staring at the moonless night. Bright stars lit the way and billowing puff clouds dominated the sky. It was a beautiful night as two stripes of colored star masses crossed over to each horizon their edges pink, white and blue.

So very beautiful that Mini had Riel look at the sky for a few moments.

Riel said, "The stars are in slightly different locations, but it is very similar to what I saw from the Islands I grew up on."

"How do you know which way to go, Riel? There is nothing but water out here. And you seem so at ease."

"It is something borne into me from the Silkies and from the sea, and then also signs from the Creator," replied Riel. "See the stars at the end of a cluster which looks like a dipper. Look where I am pointing. If you follow the two stars upward, they point to a very dim and inconsequential star close by, the first star you can see. See it?" Mini nodded. "That is the North Star. It never varies and all the stars rotate around that one star. We call it the guiding light. It is much dimmer than many other bright lights in the night sky, but it never fails to bring a sailor home. It is much like you, tiny and not bright to our eyes, but there to guide and help when the need arises."

Mini stared off into the luminescent heavens, wondering at the great God that could put all that into place. A few minutes later, two freshwater porpoises popped up, swimming alongside, laughing and calling to Riel.

"You must be Riel! We are sent to you," said the first porpoise. "We saw the Black Dragon rise and fly the Sea today and knew you would be here soon. Ha ha, we love Liam, and He told us to look for you. Do you have tow ropes?"

Mini had thoughtfully thrown in two extra ropes after scouring a few caves back at the shore just as they had prepared to leave. She could not help move the boat or set the mast, so she went looking for things that might be of use.

Mini and Riel tied up the ropes to the inside of the boat and the threw the lines into the water just as two lumbering whales bobbed to the surface right in front of the vessel. Lawrence heard the commotion and took the cloth off his face. He looked over the edge and saw one of the whales breach not a hundred feet off the bow. He started screaming an unknown and unheard-of sound until this very moment. The whales were ten times the size of the boat, and the shock wave shook the whole vessel. Uriel let out a sound of terror.

Lawrence keeled over. Uriel tried to help but was stuck in position as his weight shifted the boat. Riel managed alone and moved Lawrence's body so it was more centered.

Meanwhile, the porpoises had took the tow lines to the whales and they grabbed them with their mouths. They began undulating their massive tails in union. It took a very delicate balance. The porpoises were darting back and forth giving advice to the whales to keep the boat from being airborne. Uriel was frozen in terror in the bow, no aide to Riel who was desperately trying to keep the craft from capsizing or flipping. He would leap from this side to that, jumping over Lawrence, who never knew how lucky he was to be out of it. Mini soon got the idea and tried to balance the weight too although her efforts had very little effect.

Before the sun cleared the horizon, they had crossed the Salton Sea, more than 700 kilometers (434.6 miles). The whales and porpoises bid them farewell just as the shoreline was visible.

Riel unfurled the sail again and soon had them beached. Riel took a pail and drenched Lawrence who woke huffing and snorting, expelling water out his nose.

"I am sorry Lawrence, but we are very visible right here and we need to get moving and hide the boat," said Riel. "You have no idea what you missed."

"I sure wish I could faint like that when I was in trouble, Mule," exclaimed Uriel. "Might have saved me from a lot of scarring and wounds as well as fights I had to win."

"Boy Uriel, I would not be badgering Lawrence," said Riel. "Excuse the relational reference Mini, but YOU were not exactly helpful last night. You can't keep on with this bickering as now we have a Dragon on our tail. Lawrence's load is heavy, and he often carries me, which is helpful. He may have his faults and faint a lot, but you also have faults."

"What faults?" Uriel asked.

"Well to tell you the truth you really do stink," said Riel. "I mean, it is beyond me how you can sneak up on anything and the smell last night in the cave with the cinder. I don't think I will ever recover from that memory. And you get scared too like when Dragon came and in the boat with the whales last night. So, stop calling him a Mule and put the quest first as Liam instructed. We must get moving."

Uriel gave Lawrence a dirty look and started unpacking the supplies. He stopped at one point and again waded out into the water, but this time took a few minutes to rub his fur with wet sand.

Lawrence was soon loaded up, and the boat stowed under a large tree and covered in branches. Riel got into the saddle. Mini leaped up onto the Uriel's back, holding on between the bear's ears.

Mini fit perfectly into the space and soon found out that tugging on one ear or the other would influence where Uriel went, however this took time to develop.

"I wondered how you planned to keep up with us," Uriel said, tilting his head back and looking up between his ears. This dislodged Mini, requiring her to get back up between the ears again. Riel laughed out loud at the absurdity of it all.

The Dragon was lying in the sand, on his belly cleaning his teeth with his curved razor-sharp claws. He was on the beach in front of the building he burned out and very comfortable in the morning sun. Aragant was pacing back and forth in front of him.

"You said a marmot spoke to you here but you burned the building so you can't smell anything but smoke?" said Aragant.

"YES, again, stupid, stubborn human." The Dragon thought about the day he would be free from this man and what he was going to do. It made him smile in a nasty way. It also made him hungry.

"How about those marks in the sand? They look like a boat was launched after we left. They have got to be out on the Salton Sea." Aragant snarled in utter frustration. He took his riding crop and hit the Dragon which, of course, meant nothing on those huge scales.

"If you say so human," remarked the Dragon. In a flash of power, he suddenly lifted into the air, dived into the waves, and emerged with a huge fish in his jaws. He started gnawing on the fish's head and calmly exerted pressure on the fish skull so that it burst and exploded in his mouth. Bone fragments flew everywhere with bits of flesh and sinew still attached. A rather large fragment hit Aragant right across his chest.

"I would say hurling fish bones at me would qualify as 'DOING ME HARM,'" snarled Aragant.

"If you did not possess my name, I would do lots more than hurl fish bones at you" the Dragon answered. "After all, you think you are so smart if you think they are on the Sea."

Aragant picked up the piece of bone and threw it right at the Dragon's face. The Dragon deftly caught it, hurled it way up in the air and caught it in his jaw. He spit it out, so it landed right by Aragant's feet spewing up sand. Aragant had to stop and sneeze, but he knew who really had the upper hand. "I will mount you now Dragon and you will do a hunt for the boat using a serpentine pattern. They must be out on the water."

A few days later, Riel and his entourage were almost to the Barrier Mountains. Riel was used to riding Lawrence who had set a rather furious pace to humiliate Uriel. Uriel, however, kept circling to the front of the group and from time to time would jump out from a bush, tree, or rock scaring Lawrence who would squeal. However, Lawrence soon caught on and when Uriel disappeared from the end of the line, he would purposely take a path with the least vegetation, so Uriel had to circle wide to get in front. The game was getting more and more tricky for both players.

Ahead a broad line of huge, desolate snowy mountains broke the skyline. Many jagged peaks were lost in clouds, rain and snow swirled around their heads. The trees stopped about a quarter of the way up as the climate was too cold and merciless above in those lofty peaks. The result was sheer barren rock faces and deep crevices at impossible angles. Riel was breathless with the sheer magnitude of the place. He felt very small indeed.

"Uriel, did your family come from here or somewhere else?"

"The Filk bears came from the base of that highest peak," said Uriel. "It is said the Lord himself created us to walk the green valleys below. We were once many and strong, but Aragant and the False King have us spread far and wide. We are few now from the onslaught. I have not seen another female in the eleven years since I lost my mate and our cubs."

"But the Lord can restore you, Uriel," said Riel. "He can do things we cannot imagine. Things we do not understand because our minds and bodies are so limited."

At that exact moment, another Filk bear walked across the meadow not a mile distant. The group had just crested a hill overlooking a verdant valley. Uriel took off like a shot depositing Mini into Riel's lap in the process.

"Oh great," said Lawrence, "the bear is off investigating family ties."

"It is a female, Lawrence," replied Mini. "The females have a black band across their backs. Uriel has committed to us, and he will continue to guide us even if he is distracted for a little while. Have more thought towards your friend."

They caught up with the bears a few minutes later. Uriel was frozen in place with an undignified and silly look on his face as he stared at the female. He was stricken with her size and sheer beauty and remained sitting as the group arrived.

"Does this lump talk?" asked the female as they approached.

"Of course," replied Mini. "But we are on a quest for Liam our Lord and must set a desperate pace. Please help if you can. Judging by the look on Uriel's face, it is going to be tough getting him moving again."

She looked intrigued and said, "well, where are you going? Where did you see Liam?"

"We are going to the Isle of Paradise and Uriel is leading us," replied Riel. "This is Lawrence and Mini and I am Riel. I saw Liam and he saved Lawrence and I from Belial a few months ago. We have been traveling since. Uriel is the statue over there."

"I see," said the bear, looking very thoughtful. She glanced at Uriel who let out what might be described as a moan. "Are you taking Rippon's pass?"

"Yes, that is exactly where Liam told Uriel to take us."

"Then I will go with you to the pass. Uriel might find his voice by then. And, by the way, I am Fammy."

Fammy was huge for a female but still Uriel was taller, broader, and wider. She took off on a seldom used game trail that led up the steep mountainside in a series of switchbacks. Uriel had never used this trail, but he obediently followed Fammy as if he had been tied on a leash.

The next day as they broke camp high up the mountainside, Riel felt a cold shiver go down his back. He looked at the clouds and the blue sky and tried to shake it off. However, as they were eating breakfast, he felt it again but this time it felt more focused and near, like an evil thing was looking at them. He turned to Fammy and said, "I just had a real bad shiver thing go down my body. I've never felt that before. Does it mean anything?"

Mini and Fammy both got a terrified look on their faces.

"Quickly, don't leave a trace in this camp. The Dragon is near! But hopefully, he has not seen us yet. If we hurry, we can take shelter in that cave back a few hundred yards," cried Mini. Fammy jumped into action, and Riel cleaned the camp as quickly as he could. Lawrence stood shaking and crying as Riel loaded him with alacrity. Mini jumped onto Lawrence's back and he followed the bears down the track. Riel, his arms loaded down with bags and food, followed running. They all ran into a deep cavern just as, high up on the loftiest peak, a dark shadow passed.

The Dragon flew over the mountain and landed in the very meadow where the bears met each other. He was very hungry and more than a little out of sorts. After flying over the Sea for hours with that thing on his back demanding he keep going back and forth, he only wanted to rip Aragant's body to pieces.

"There is no way they got this far," said Aragant. "They could not have crossed that Sea so quickly."

"So, I take it you have extraordinary sight, exceptional hearing, and the ability to fly? Or could it be that Dragons are equipped with things humans only dream about? Oh yes, you are ARAGANT, I forgot."

Using the Dragon's real name, Aragant said, "So okay, why did you bring us here then?"

The Dragon cringed and looked around the meadow to make sure no one heard his name. "Walk lightly human, if another hears my name, they may be able to free me from you. Not all can withstand my gaze."

"I am so afraid!" Aragant chuckled under his breath. "I command you under the power of your name, never to physically harm me. Since you are under my power you cannot break what you have spoken. Now speak it aloud."

The Dragon began to rock his head back and forth. His tail was slapping a nearby boulder. He looked directly at Aragant and started his hypnotic stare but Aragant just shook it off after a few moments. He was forced to promise but Dragons have ways of manipulating words to their benefit. He said, "As time and words bind, this Dragon will not do harm to this man's body. By my name I promise this." However, the Dragon relished the thought of playing with this man's mind. The only way the two-legged thing could withstand his stare for a few seconds was because the man knew his name. Yet, for now, he remained bound. One day that would end. When he finished his promise, his tail hit the boulder with such force it exploded, and he took out a nearby fir tree. The Dragon moved just as he did this to protect the fragile man. Aragant leaped slightly but held his ground giving Dragon a dirty look.

The man repeated, "so why are we here?"

"I have seen evidence from the air of travelers. They are ahead of us," said the Dragon.

"How do you know it is them?"

"Donkeys have an especially delicious scent and even now I can smell one having passed this meadow. How many donkeys are out here in the Barrier Mountains, human?"

"I don't believe it. How could they get this far ahead of us?"

"Just remember that Liam is involved," the Dragon answered. "When HE gets involved, you know things are not just simple. I have not seen them from the air, although the clouds were obscuring my gaze. But I felt them, somewhere on this mountain. You could let me scent them out by myself and I could track them for you."

"I am not so stupid as to let you out of my sight or even very far away. Now where could they be going in these mountains? How many passes are there above?"

"Eight."

"How many are accessible from this spot in particular?" Aragant asked. "Anything else I should know since you only give me exactly what I ask? Details this time."

"Four, but two are extremely dangerous and not good for donkeys or bears. It is easy to watch the first two from that peak to your left. But it is incredibly cold up there, not suitable for men like you." The Dragon could not help but let out a little snarl and bare his teeth at Aragant. The man ignored him.

"Oh yes, I am going to follow a Dragon's advice for sure," said Aragant. "A beast who never exactly tells the exact truth but only as much as is necessary.   You just want me to freeze into your blessed uncomfortable saddle. It has left a permanent imprint on my frame. No, we are going to use our resources. By now my men are crossing the Salton Sea and should have a camp set up by the time we fly back. I am hungry, tired, and stiff from your boney scales imprinting my arms and legs. We are going to return. I'm getting a hot meal and decent night's sleep and you can place my men above to watch the four passes tomorrow morning."

The Dragon was elated because as Aragant made that decision, he watched Lawrence dart out of a cave high above, more than halfway up the mountain and just below the most dangerous pass. The man had forgot to ask about their whereabouts, or he would have had to tell him under the power of his own name. It felt very good indeed to trick the human and keep him from his quarry. The smell of their bodies made his stomach turn and this one had ridden him for days.

The whole time they stayed in the cave, Uriel and Fammy became more and more nervous and agitated. Mini looked out the entrance and far below she could just make up the form of a Dragon in the very meadow the bears met in. It started to feel colder and colder near the entrance. The bears both agreed that terrible weather was on the way, but the pass was very near and there were some hours of daylight left. They decided as a group to chance heading up. Lawrence went first but neglected to let Mini signal him as he ran to hide behind the nearest rock.

That was the only time the Dragon was facing the right direction and he did not react. So, the others waited until

Mini signaled when the Dragon's back was facing them. A few minutes later, hidden behind a tower of boulders, Mini looked back to see the Dragon looking directly at them. She let out a scream which echoed off the rocks and valley nearby. Everyone scrambled for cover. Mini could just make out the Dragon's wide smile as the man mounted his back and a few minutes later she realized their nemesis was heading back to the Salton Sea but she could not explain why. It bothered her the rest of the day.

"I tell you Uriel, that Dragon saw us back there. Dragons can be very tricky at keeping their word if the commands are not exact. Still, I know I saw him scenting us and has revealed that we are here in these mountains. He must know there are only four passes. Why would they flying back when he could have eaten us all? Why was he smiling when Aragant mounted him? None of this is making sense at all. I do know one thing."

Uriel took the bait. "What is that Mini?"

"We have a window to cross the pass, but it must be today," Mini said. "We must make haste and get to the other side as distance is hardly a problem for the winged serpent. They know we are here, but they will have to watch all four passes. Hopefully, if we can cross before they get here, perhaps they will not watch the other side. The Salton's quick crossing probably confused Aragant. Pray our luck or blessings hold for a few more hours."

Uriel, never being able to see very far, replied, "Perhaps the Dragon did not see us. The pass is two hours ahead and if we are not there by nightfall, we will lose the boy in the cold. I feel the chill of the storm even now. My skin is tingling with it, and I can feel hibernation's touch coming as well. We must press on as quickly as possible."

It was decided that Riel should ride on Fammy's back as it lightened Lawrence's load and gave him more speed. The slope got steeper and steeper as clouds swirled past them. It was cold one minute and the sun would shine, and it turned warm again. It got colder and colder as they climbed until Riel halted the procession to put on the fur jacket Liam had purchased for him back in Kruche. It was folded neatly and tightly inside the bottom of a pack. The group had to stop while it was retrieved as the terrain was so steep it was hard to get the bag off Lawrence. Riel moved quickly and was glad he had also put the fur lined boots in the same bag. The bears were dancing with impatience as Riel made sure the pack was evenly weighted on Lawrence and put the jacket and boots on. It was no easy feat as Riel moved, rocks slid off the path and dropped thousands of feet clanging and announcing their whereabouts. "Thank God, the Dragon is not around," exclaimed Riel.

They immediately took off again, Lawrence, well-practiced in following footsteps, held the incredible pace the Uriel and Fammy set. An hour and a half later, the path divided into a Y. The bears and Mini were in a heated debate.

"We take the quickest path," said Uriel when Lawrence could hear over the swirling wind. "It was I who was charged by Liam to take the boy. We go right."

"Will Lawrence be able to cross the ice bridge? I don't think so," exclaimed Mini." In a whisper that only Fammy and Mini could hear, Uriel said, "That is the quickest learning, most obstinate, most agile Mule I have ever seen. He kept up with me over the Marshes. We go right to the ice bridge and the quickest route."

"Did he?" questioned both Fammy and Mini in unison looking shocked.

"I can take part of his load, if you take Riel and Mini on your back, Uriel. I feel a great need to push ahead and go through as quickly as possible," injected Fammy.

At the Y, the path widened before going through two sheer rock columns fifty feet tall.

Riel and Mini removed most of Lawrence's load with ropes and harnesses attached it to Fammy. Riel climbed up on Uriel's back and tied a rope around his chest to help him hang on. Mini took her place between Uriel's ears, careful not to tug on either one. Lawrence was situated between the two bears and true to his stubborn self, kept his nose down, and his eyes glued to Uriel's swaying rear. Sway it did at an incredible pace through a shale field, across a relatively easy but icy valley, and then zigged up a vertical cliff on a small shelf. Uriel had huge claws and pads that assisted him up the narrow goat path, but Lawrence was another story.

Lawrence kept saying, "Liam help me! Liam HELP me!" Every step took them higher, the drop to his right was now more than a thousand feet when they finally crossed between a house-sized giant boulder which had split in half. On the other side, lay an ice field that only been used by mountain sheep as the route wound across the ice sheet with chasms on both sides. The wind had kicked up and it was getting colder and colder. Slowly they wound through the ice, with only one true slip by Lawrence but what lay ahead was much worse.

Finally, they had attained the breaks; a thirty-foot-long packed ice bridge stood between them and Rippon's Pass. The problem was the packed foot-wide path had steep slopes down on both sides into valleys far below, and no sure certain grip for a Donkey. The wind picked up again as there was no protection between the rock towers at either end.

Lawrence achieved an octave that only cold, stress and exhaustion could produce when he cried out, "Liam I am not going to make it!" He burst into tears, also a new Donkey expression. Water literally started dripping off his chin. It froze in place and gave him a set of snow whiskers.

Riel dismounted Uriel and grabbed Lawrence's lead. Fammy, Mini and Uriel crossed but it was perilous as a chunk of ice let go and crashed down the slope. Riel looked deep into Lawrence's eyes, and said, "Lawrence, I want you to just look at my back and follow my steps exactly. You've done that for many miles already and this is no different. I am going to walk in front of you just look at my back and my footprints and nothing else." Lawrence began to shake but when Riel stepped out, he tentatively put a hoof on the bridge. The bears had done their best to flatten the top ice and stood watching from the rock cropping at the other end. Lawrence started screaming when he inadvertently looked down but his whole body was committed to the crossing, and he could not back up.

Riel was glad for the skin and fur boots as it insulated his feet from the rising cold. It was a magnificent place if they had not been in such terrible danger. Far to either side, a vista of unparalleled beauty unfolded: mountain peaks to the horizon on one side and the distant Salton Sea to the other. They were truly at the top of the world. A band of dark threatening clouds chased them, and the winds suddenly changed direction. Lawrence stumbled slightly as he adjusted his weight. He let out a squeal so high pitched it hurt Mini's ears. But he was more than halfway across.

The ice below Riel's foot gave a little and he wiggled to keep his balance too. Lawrence felt panic crawl up his spine until he glanced ahead and saw Liam standing behind the bears curling his index finger and holding a big juicy carrot in the other hand. Riel stepped forward and Lawrence felt a little confidence fill his heart, and the thought of a fresh fat carrot had an impact too. They were totally exposed between the rock towers. The leading edge of the storm was almost upon them, and the air churned with the coming snow not 100 feet away. Riel looked back and said, "Lawrence, you only have a few feet to go, don't hesitate anymore!" With that encouragement Lawrence gave it his last effort.

They had crossed the breaks, and Rippon's pass just as the storm broke. Lawrence stopped to get the carrot but chewed as he ran behind the receding bears. The snow started swirling as they came out of the pass and saw a downslope path which didn't present any problem after what they had just experienced. The path was much wider and far less icy. It was still dangerous but going downhill was so much faster. The storm chased them on for another mile but dissipated when they dropped into the next valley.

They were well into a forest the next morning, when Riel began to "feel" the Dragon again: They had stopped below a dense growth of trees when Riel's breath shortened, and his heart began racing.

Far above terrified men were being Dragon dropped at the passes. He had taken pleasure in showing them his teeth before he allowed the men to ride on his back. Little did the men know their lives were in danger for nothing. The Dragon deposited some of them near Rippon's Pass, killing two of them because of limited visibility. They stepped off the Dragon's back into nothingness as they dismounted. Their screams were heard as they bounced off the sheer rock faces. Far below, the escaping party could hear their last echos even with the wind whipping through the dark trees.

THE GUARDS AT THE GATE

"Then he brought me out by way of the gate northward,
And led me round by the way without unto the outer gate,
by way of the gate that looked toward the east:
and behold, there ran waters on the right side."
Ezekiel 47:2

The next day they got an early start. They entered a deep, long, and narrow valley just as Uriel began to let off a series of huffing sounds. Fammy kept talking to him, but he just kept making strange noises and walking.

Riel finally stopped the group and stood right in front of Uriel. He gently placed his hands on Uriel's cheeks and said, "What is bothering you, my friend?"

Uriel looked sadly down at the ground then up into Riel's face, he was slightly cross eyed. "Well, if you must know, I am not exactly sure how to get to the Gates of Paradise. You must understand that no human has ever passed through those gates to the island in the lake beyond. The gates are manned by huge, winged creatures, which are terrible to behold. They are part of the living mountain, part reality and part of the spirit world, if you can understand that. They weigh the hearts of those who wish to cross into Paradise and if there is found any wrong, their bodies are burnt to fine ashes. The gaze of the creatures incinerates."

Riel dropped his hands. "Listen, Liam would never leave us stranded and alone in this wilderness, nor send us out on a useless expedition, if there was not a reason which we fail to understand right now. Look at what we have gone through to get here. He told you to personally escort me, right Uriel?"

"Well, yes, Liam told me to be with you and take you," said Uriel. "We will have to get as far as I can take you and see what happens."

A few hours later, they turned into a much narrower long but lush, verdant valley. As they got near the far end, they could see what appeared to be four huge wings imprinted on a distant granite cliff. They were two hundred feet tall and fifty feet wide. But there were no bodies attached to them and they appeared to be floating in the rock.

The trail's last half mile was sheer granite one half mile high. Their surface looked as if someone had sanded it down to an even surface between the floating wings

The last quarter mile a strange thing began to happen: As they approached each of the wing sets changed as if they were coming out of the cliff. Soon incredible giant human women bodies began to appear and every step they took closer to the gate at the end of the valley brought another feature into view.

By the time they were 100 feet from the end, the full incredible design was visible.

Riel took one more step and thunder filled the valley, and the women completely stepped out of the granite and their beautiful faces looked down on the tiny group below them. Their eyes were bright blue with blazing flashes of light and their gold crowns sparkled in the late afternoon sun.

They were still made of granite including their swirling full-length robes, but their faces were now flexible, and they stared at the new intruders. All of them had a weapon in one hand and a shield in the other, still all made of rock. The narrow space between the middle two figures held the metal latching gate which exited to a narrow dark canyon with sheer rock faces on both sides. It was as if the water, over a millennia before, drained through that small channel and carved a path just wide enough for a horse, or bear in this case.

Uriel stopped them there and went up to the first angel's granite robe and touched it.

It was solid rock. He stepped back and said, "Now, what do we do? We are all tired, let's just make camp and hope for a break or some instructions."

Riel was looking up mesmerized. He felt the being's dangerous but non-malignant presence. He was still looking up into their eyes a few minutes later when he heard Lawrence exclaim, "good grief, they dwarf all of us! What are we going to do if Aragant and his Dragon find us boxed in here." As is normal, he looked terrified and started shaking.

"Perhaps we might stop and think to worship and pray here. I will get the camp set- up but then I will need time to pray and discern what Liam wants us to do. We are all in a dangerous place, but we are stepping in the Lord's will and that is never wrong," said Riel. It was a warm and balmy afternoon, and the last shafts of sun were hitting the valley floor as the camp was established. The grass was thick, dotted with azure, gold, and blue wildflowers, wildly fragrant in the wafting breezes. The company fell into a mellow mood whispering among themselves. Soon they were all asleep in the grass except for Riel who was kneeling a little distance from the gate praying.

Liam entered from the other side of the gate walking in the thick grass towards Riel and said, "You have done well Riel."

Riel, turned, let out a cry of delight and ran to Liam who scooped him up in his broad arms, rotating so Riel's legs swung out in a wide circle. Riel started weeping. Liam started laughing.

"Liam, Liam, where did you go?" Riel asked. "I thought I could not make it after that huge Dragon thing burnt the derelict house to the ground. Poor Lawrence was so scared, and the bears have been tireless companions. I don't know how to get past these huge angel things and none of the animals know either. I just feel so dirty and smelly as we have not stopped or rested well in weeks now. It was terrible with the whales and the boat almost capsized. Please, can I stay here in your arms for a few minutes?"

Liam sat down on the grass and held Riel so he was rocking against his chest in his arms. Liam gently stroked Riel's hair. He began to whisper in Riel's ear. "I have been with you the whole way, son. I understand what you have accomplished because I have commanded it. You have made it to here and I am here to help you now. You will be the only child of God to have passed into Eden and the Isle of Paradise without having died. You left your Island far behind as a boy, but you will pass this gate as a formidable man. You chose to pray rather than try to enter.

"You brought our Lawrence through to here even though he is very scared and faints a lot, but he is so courageous too! These things and so many more will make you a true leader of men."

Riel searched Liam's face. "Are the animals going through the gate?"

"Yes, they are. However, it seems they need a little nap before we start through the gate in the morning." Liam laughed because Lawrence and Uriel were actually touching their rear ends together and Lawrence's legs were straight up in the air, his hooves drooping over his body. He was dreaming something and quivered and quaked with his dreamland adventure. A moment later he rolled onto his side cuddling up against Uriel's warm furry back. Both Liam and Riel laughed.

"Let's make them a little warm food and wake them all in an hour," said Liam. "There is a nice berry patch nearby and the bears will have a hearty feast of them. I brought fresh carrots and some meat even for you. We will make a nice stew and I am sure they will be surprised. But before that, why don't you just relax here on my chest and just take some deep breaths." They sat watching the others sleep for a few minutes as the sun dipped over the edge of the canyon.

An hour later, a boiling pot of stew was hung over the open fire, a fresh carrot was put right beside Lawrences quivering nose, and Riel got a nice pot of berries for each of the bears. Mini got a pot of seeds and a few fresh strawberries.   O n e of Lawrence's eyes opened as the realization that his nose was sniffing fresh produce. He spotted Liam and Riel, letting out a sudden scream. That woke the whole lot of them.

It was a cacophony of cries, tears and joy as the animals realized who had appeared. Lawrence took off bucking and prancing, the bears grabbed each other and rolled on the grass, Mini started dancing and singing, and Riel just watched in amusement. There was sheer joy in the air.

After everyone calmed down, and they had eaten, Liam said, "I know all of you are bursting with questions, however, I must tell you what is going to happen when the sun rises tomorrow morning, so you all are ready to go. Tomorrow is the one day of the year when the sun is perfectly lines up with the path through the gate and between the guardian angel's robes. A ray of light will touch the gate, I will cover Riel with my robe and open the gate for all of you. You need to pass quickly through. Riel will be the only human in history to have passed the Gate without death accompanying him. You all, even our Mini will be known through the ages for having protected and helped him to get here."

They all sat around the campfire for another hour asking questions and thinking about what would happen in the morning. The moon came up and a bright band of stars sung in the heavens above them. Soon they all began to yawn and took their places near the fire as the night had turned slightly chilly except for Uriel and Fammy, who had taken to sleeping in each other's arms at some distance from the fire.

Early the next morning, excitement gripped the group as they packed up the camp, this time leaving remnants of the fire, bits of food and tracks to the gate. It was thirty minutes before the sun gained the horizon and they were all practically dancing in anticipation. The towering angels had exchanged their weapons somehow in the night for huge trumpets and their appearance changed as the minutes elapsed. Their robes became shining white cloth that glimmered with light; their features became flesh and blood and the trumpets turned to pure gold. They began a strange sort of talking between themselves and they stepped in unison completely out of the cliff face. It was almost audible to Riel but Mini heard the sounds clearly. A few minutes before the event, the Angel's put the instruments to their lips and all four of them stood at the ready. The pre-dawn light revealed that Liam had a strange blood-stained white robe on, and crown made of thorns, small rivulets of blood coursed down his face.

Riel was going to ask why but then the sun burst over a distant mountain's notch and a bright, golden shaft of hot, white light hit the Gate and illuminated the further canyon. Just then, the trumpets sounded in unison and then began a musical composition so beautiful that Liam had to holler for the animals to move through. They were already lined up, so it did not take long before Liam helped Riel hide quickly under his lengthy robe. They managed an ungainly walk through the gate as Riel was completely blind inside the cloth. It smelled badly of sweat and blood and Riel was almost gagging. The Gate slammed shut behind them and then the angels turned to granite and began disintegrating and crumbling apart. All four of them were reduced to boulders and sharp stones, blocking the gate, and filling in the first few feet of opening beyond.

The entry was sealed shut.

Liam lifted the edge of his robe and Riel stepped out, but a chocking dust caused them to move down a few hundred yards. They all had to line up in single file to fit in the narrow channel. Uriel was in trouble as both his sides hit the walls. He had to take a breath, expel it, and move a few feet forward. However, in three hundred yards the channel began to widen and soon they were making headway. A half a mile further and the channel suddenly ended at a shoreline. A dock jutted out into the crystal-clear water and the most perfectly formed and beautiful woman stood waiting for them in a boat just big enough for all of them. Liam waved at her, and she smiled at him. Her long black hair was tied in an elegant braid. Her eyes were bright blue, but her skin and teeth were blinding white. She let out a cry of joy when she saw Riel.

Liam said, "Go to her Riel, that is your real mother, Adriel. She sacrificed everything to meet you here. You must not touch her in any fashion. The rest of us will wait here while you have a few minutes to talk." Riel walked to the boat and took a seat facing his mother. He couldn't speak for a few minutes but eventually they began a conversation.

In the meantime, a bent, terribly old man with dark skin wrinkled into many folds, approached Liam on the shore. He had on a white sparkling robe like the angels in the cliff. He used an oar to help him stumble up to the animals.

"AH! Soon this will be your last crossing my faithful companion. I have come to take you at last," exclaimed Liam.

"The gate is closed, and the path is shut to Paradise. The Prophecy has come to pass.

"You are forbidden to touch any of my companions or Riel." Liam pointed to the boy in the boat. "They are still in reality and the only ones to gain Heaven without you accompanying them to the Isle. You may not take anyone else across by this avenue again. I will return and retrieve you later, but you are free to rest here until I return."

"As you command," replied the elderly man in an unusually loud and powerful voice.

Mini jumped up the cloth of Liam's robe and sat on his shoulder. "Who is that Liam? Why is your robe covered in blood and sweat and you have that nasty crown of thorns on your head?"

Liam laughed out loud. He threw the crown of thorns down the path and walked to end of the pier, stripped off the robe, entangling Mini, and jumped into the lake. He retrieved Mini a moment later as the water was only waist deep.

Then he rubbed Mini from head to toe with the water and set her back on the pier. He dived into the water and came up a few yards out from the surprised animals. Lawrence was the first one to jump in and start splashing. The rest soon followed suit. They all cavorted and played games but then took the opportunity to bathe.

Liam got out of the water and the old man handed him a new white glimmering robe which he put on.

Death handed Liam the oar and sat down on a nearby chair-sized flattop rock. They all headed to the boat together with Liam in the lead. Mini had got up on Liam's shoulder, her new perch.

"Why is the guy with the oar so old, Liam," inquired Mini.

"He is not young or old. He is Death. Sometimes he is a child, a young man but sometimes he appears ancient. He is ancient today because I have brought Riel through the Gate."

Mini said, "Why did you have to bring Riel through the Gate?"

"I had to cover Riel with my robe because the angels only let men through who have no sin and are perfect. Riel, as good as he is, has still said and done things that were wrong.

"I had to make him invisible to the angels, I posted them as guards at the gate. So, I covered him in my robe from another place and time where I had to make my life the sacrifice to cover all their sins. You animals all passed because you do not know the way of sin, so you passed uncovered and in my company. Now the Gate is shut between reality and Isle of Paradise. Men may only enter by accepting grace, asking for redemption, repenting, and walking with me, and when they die, they cross into Heaven."

"Riel said the angels had tears in their eyes when they saw you. Why?" inquired Mini. "They have stood at that Gate since the dawn of created man," said Liam. "When I appeared at the Gate, they knew they only had a few short hours left to stand guard. Look, they are already on the Isle. You can just see them in the distance."

Mini held her tiny paws over her eyes and saw them standing on the further shore. Adriel exited the boat and went to stand beside Death. She helped him up and they began walking along the shoreline towards the island. Liam would pick them up later further down the shore.

The animals, Liam and Riel entered the boat. Riel sat in the prow, Lawrence sat sideways behind him, and each bear took up the remaining two benches. Mini was still on Liam's shoulder. As they left the dock with Liam poling the boat, a strange grey mist formed behind them in the narrows and near the dock area. It gathered and swirled around making tendrils which eventually formed into two angels like the ones at the Gate. These were even bigger beings dressed in linen undergarments, short-sleeved bright-blue tunics, leather trousers, greaves, mail armor, arm guards, and a feathered Coolus helmet. With their rugged handsome faces drawn tight with effort, they swung their mighty axes in unison and began busting down the cliffs and destroying the dock. The sound was deafening. The mists continued to build, the clouds of debris and dust gathered and soon all was obscured from sight.

Riel leaned over the front of the boat looking down into the water. "Why are there bright colored stars and swirling light cloud things in the water, Liam?"

"We are passing over time itself Riel," said Liam. "The spirals are very far away galaxies. You notice they appear to be moving? It is not them moving but us. No one can cross the Crystal Sea without death or me accompanying them. Now all of you listen carefully to me. Do not go to the other side of the island. Stay only on the shore where we land or enter the circular wood door into the hill. Anything you say will come true. There is nothing in Paradise that is not true so be very careful before you talk, this includes you Lawrence and especially you Uriel." He gave Uriel a stare and Uriel looked away.

The Dragon let out a loud cry when Aragant snapped his whip and hit his open eye. It stung for a brief period, but his inner eyelid had closed and so the damage was more in the line of embarrassment. It cemented his hatred of man even deeper. Aragant was frothing at the mouth in utter rage. The Dragon had twisted suddenly when the whip hit him, and the man almost lost his balance except for the tight security belt on his waist. That made Aragant even more angry.

"You are an incompetent, useless, flying piece of useless flesh. You almost dropped me, and I see the Gate to Paradise destroyed below! My GOD! The boy has crossed in." Far below a thick heavy grey cloud bank obscured all vision beyond the gate.

"Land! Land you useless flying hunk of nothing!" (Many other words were used to describe the Dragon but cannot be repeated in good company.) "YOU did this to me! If only you had done exactly as I told you!

"My two missing guards were not there to stop them because you let them off into open air."

"You only told me to DROP them off," answered the Dragon. "Not drop them off SAFELY and I landed on Rippon's

Pass in a cloud cover. They dismounted without looking." The Dragon's evil smile was telling. "Besides Riel had already crossed over before we got there."

Aragant screamed with frustration. "WHAT?"

"I told you they were in front of us. You chose not to believe me. I could smell all of them and they had been there a few hours before."

"Why didn't you tell me? You are a conniving, feral, useless piece of garbage?"

"I do as you command Aragant. I do not have to do any more than that. And if I don't get fed soon you are not going to be flying anywhere," the Dragon answered.

They landed in front of the pile of sharp debris that once held the Gate. Aragant looked disgusted when he realized the Liam's camp was undisturbed and that they had not even tried to disguise it. The cloud bank above the remaining cliff was so thick it was black in places. "Well, we are defeated for now, but this is not the end. No thanks to you! I think another session in your chains back with the nuns is in order. I will personally take delight in whipping you afterward."

"Okay, I will get some sleep then and not have to be your pack animal," the Dragon answered. "Sounds good. With my eyes closed there is nothing you can do to hurt me, so I look forward to it. Perhaps I might consume or kill a few more of your men on the way." A terrible snarl followed.

In Paradise the comrades exited the boat onto the Island. Riel thought the crossing would take a few minutes, but it was such slow going it ended up taking hours. The passage took so long Riel's neck hurt from staring at the stars and galaxies leaning over the bow. He was thinking about the incredible colors and lights. Liam looked at him, air brushed a finger over his neck and the pain was gone.

For once, Lawrence had not fainted crossing the water, but when he got out, he let out a sigh of relief and laid down on the grass. Uriel decided to taunt him.

"Too bad you couldn't experience our sea voyages without going dark Donkey."

Lawrence turned into a black Donkey. He jumped so hard he ended up standing. "What have you done to me Uriel?"

"Well, that is a lot better Lawrence, but I think Liam prefers you back the way you were as a Donkey." Uriel guffawed as again Lawrence bucked when he returned to his original color.

"Don't you ever listen to Liam? What is the matter with you bears? You should cross Rippon's pass in my body and see how it feels." replied Lawrence.

POP! Then a BOOM and both bears suddenly disappeared.

"STOP! STOP IT! Now both bears must cross Rippon's Pass as donkeys. Can you imagine how hard that is going to be? You must all be very careful what you say from here on. Now all of you go into that door in the hillside and get something to eat and rest until I can retrieve them. Practice SILENCE!" Liam looked slightly disgusted and rolled his eyes.

Riel, who was not a part of the current disaster, said, "Where are the bears? Are they crossing the pass as donkeys?" He was looking at Liam.

"Reality and the spirit world are together from this heavenly perspective," said Liam. "The bears are physically at the pass as donkeys. They must go across to complete the truth and I can retrieve them then. They are not happy or charmed by you Lawrence but perhaps they might have more mercy towards you in the future. Uriel especially. When you are physically in the real world, it is very, very difficult to perceive the spirit world, but it surrounds you. It is like looking into a mirror with dark, broken, dirty glass. There are ways to see it: prayer, stepping forward in faith, receiving the gift of prophecy, and simply letting my spirit work in your hearts. It becomes clearer and more solid the closer you become to me."

Riel walked to the door in the hill and motioned for the rest to follow. Liam disappeared as soon as Riel turned away.

On Rippon's Pass Liam motioned to Uriel who was one giant donkey with brown hair. The bear-donkey combination was halfway across the frozen ridge, but Uriel was frozen and shaking in terror. Fammy was already across. She said, "God Liam, how does that donkey navigate?"

Liam said, "Uriel, all you must do is cross this last twenty feet! You are already halfway across! Just take a few more steps. Come on, you can do this and as soon as you get here, I can take you back in your bear body."

Uriel looked up at Liam but, unfortunately, had looked down just before Liam spoke to him. In the clear air, the drop below looked even worse than it had when they crossed before. It was a clear sunny day and a chunk of ice had just broken free below Uriel's hoof and he had just managed to recover. He looked longingly at Liam.

"I can't do it Liam. It feels all wrong and my balance is off." He let off a scream that caused a few boulders below to roll off a ledge.

They crashed down the mountainside sending shock waves up Uriel's spine.

"Uriel, just look at me," said Liam. "Take a step and look at me. Take another and look at me. I am here with you, and you can do this."

Uriel took a few more steps but covered the rest by literally leaping the last five feet. A huge ice chunk broke free, and a part of the ridge suddenly cracked and then broke off. The piece crashed and bounced downhill, hitting another rock shelf which also broke free and soon the whole side of the mountain was sliding down along an enormous snowfield causing an avalanche. It took some minutes for the commotion to stop below.

Uriel safely reformed as a bear, watched over the lip of the cliff safely behind Liam's shoulder. "Is that ever going to stop? I'm never calling him a Mule again."

Liam smiled. "Perhaps you really are a reformed bear. Nothing like walking a paltry 50 feet in another's moccasins or in this case, hoofs. I would suggest that until you leave Paradise, you just keep your mouth shut." All three re-appeared on the Isle of Paradise.

The bears were both exhausted and horribly hungry. The group entered the door left open for them.

Inside a party was going full tilt. Everyone was singing and dancing. The Hall was hung with bunting, streamers, and decorated with flowers. Huge bouquets of blue, yellow, fuchsia, and white flowers were along the edges of the hall and on every table. There were no windows, but the hall seemed to be full of light, everything seemed to be bright and colorful. Mini ran up and got on Liam's shoulder.

She whispered into Liam's ear, "Liam, why did you leave Riel and let us take him to the Gate?"

Liam said, "You must let children go and let them grow. He would not be able to do what he needs to or have the knowledge or wisdom to live with this evil generation without these experiences. Also, it gives him choice. But now he has the strength to go forward and reach his full potential."

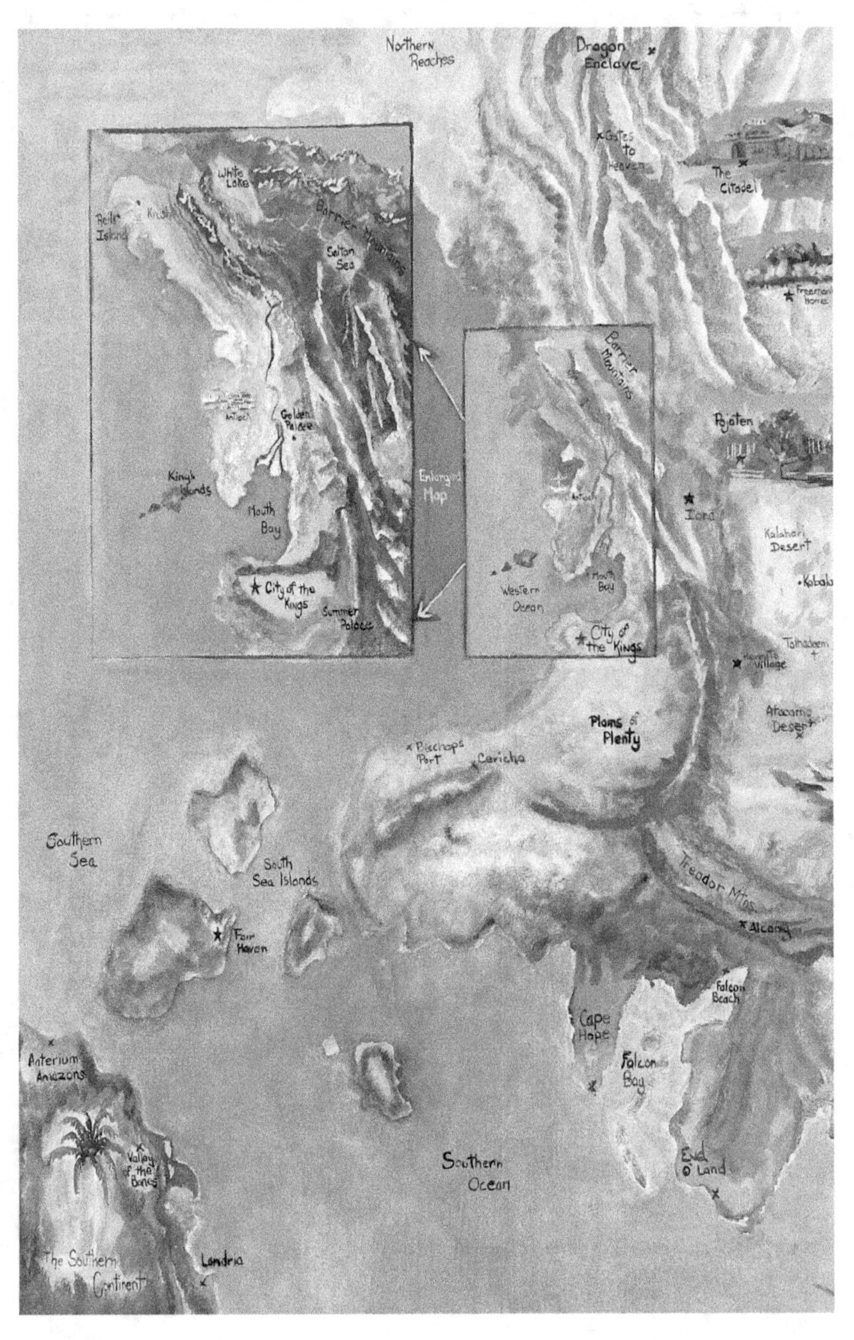
Northern Reaches
Dragon Enclave
Gates to Heaven
The Citadel
White Lake
Barrier Mountains
Knish
Reils Island
Selton Sea
Freeman Homes
Artofi
Golden Palace
Pajaten
Iona
Enlarged Map
Barrier Mountains
Kalahari Desert
King's Islands
Mouth Bay
Artofi
Kobala
City of the Kings
Summer Palace
Western Ocean
Mouth Bay
Talhadeen
Village
City of the Kings
Atacama Desert
Plains of Plenty
Bischops Port
Cericho
Southern Sea
South Sea Islands
Treador Mtns.
Alcania
Fair Haven
Falcon Beach
Cape Hope
Anterium Amazons
Falcon Bay
Valley of the Bones
End O' Land
Southern Ocean
The Southern Continent
Landria

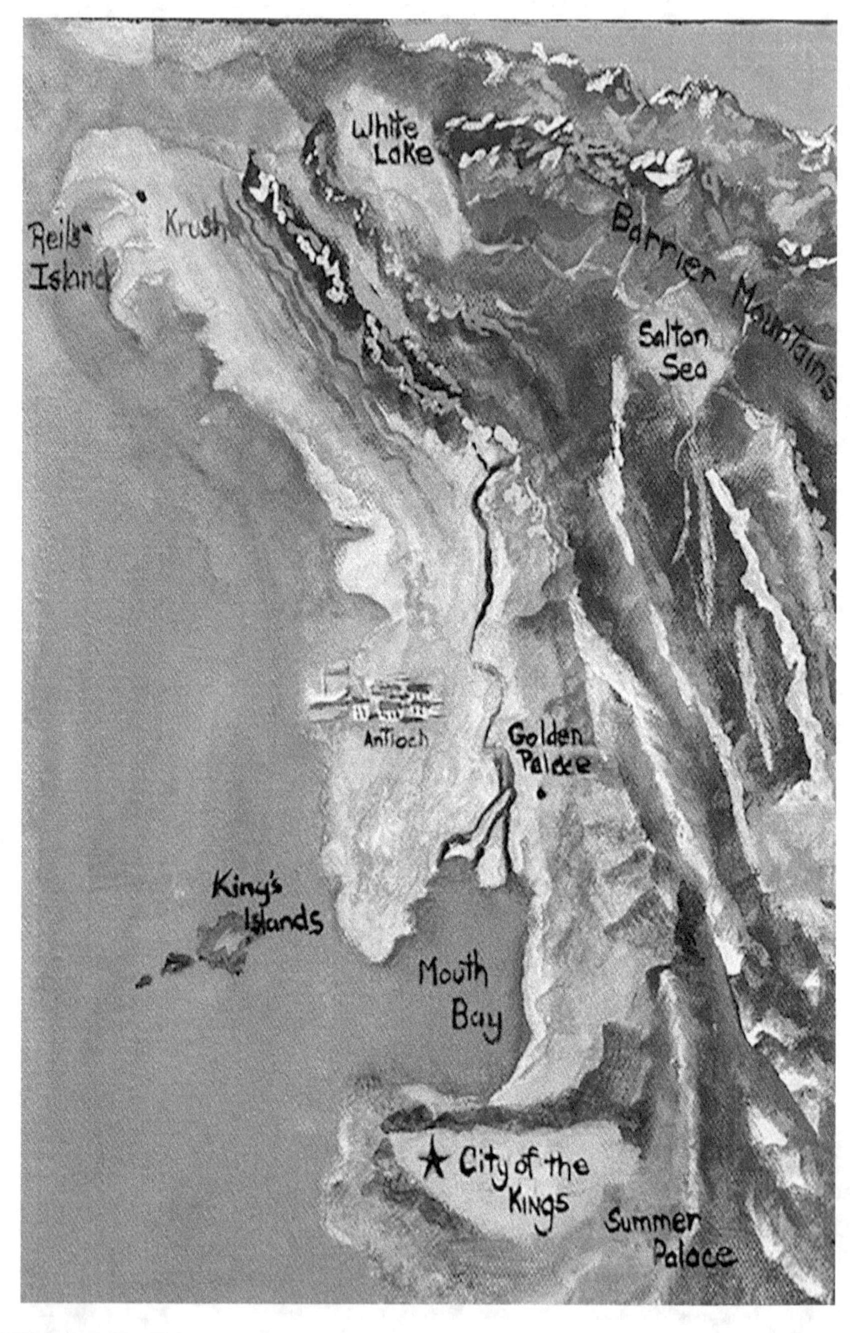

White Lake
Reils Island
Krush
Barrier Mountains
Salton Sea
Antioch
Golden Palace
King's Islands
Mouth Bay
City of the Kings
Summer Palace

11

RETURNED

*"For you were going astray like sheep;
but are now returned unto the Shepherd
and Bishop of your souls."*
I Peter 2:25.

The sun was on the horizon and the evergreen trees cast long shadows across the troupe sleeping in the meadow. In the center of them all Riel Ran Agam slept peacefully, his face held a look of pure bliss.

Mini was the first to open her eyes. She shook her head, stood up, and then stretched her long body, revealing a set of long dagger-like teeth.

She looked around and was surprised to be back in the real world again. The colors were much duller and the light totally wrong for Paradise.

They were in a grassy, emerald, green bowl surrounded by tall, jagged granite mountains again.

But these mountains did not look or feel like the Barrier Peaks.

Tiny compact flowers of every hue lived in the crooks and crannies of the mountainside and continued down to the grassy slope they were laying on. Nearby a small turquoise pond surround by tall grass rippled in the morning breeze.

Mini walked over to Lawrence. She could not believe her eyes. The Donkey's coat had changed from soft brown and grey to a stark pattern of black and white stripes. He was bigger and his shiny stand-up, black mane accentuated his whole new coat. Mini had to circle around him twice, stopping to look closely at his face. Yes, it was the Lawrence but so much more handsome with his new look. She touched his face with her tiny paw. He slowly opened one eye then the other, yawning all the while.

Lawrence stood up and said, "OH no! It's all wrong! Where are we?"

Mini responded, "Obviously we are back in reality Lawrence. But look at yourself! You are black and white and much bigger."

While Mini was talking, Lawrence was staring at her. "What happened to you Mini?"

"What?" asked Mini.

"You are bigger too but you coat is so beautiful. It has spots and tiny stripes of a darker color underneath. You are kind of amber colored with brown spots bordered by a black circle. It is incredible."

Mini and Lawrence ignored the others who were still sleeping and went to the pond to look. The reflections revealed different, larger animals with fine glossy coats.

"When I get home, I will be the talk of the barn." Lawrence pranced around the pond splashing and looking at his reflection. He bounded a few times in pure joy.

Riel stood up rubbing his sleepy eyes. "Where are we?"

Uriel and Fammy rolled over on their backs and opened their eyes.

"We are back Riel. I'm trying to remember Heaven, but it seems to be a dream and I am losing the details. I don't know what is going on," replied Mini still wet from the pond.

Both bears stood up and stretched. Riel looked at the bears and reached for his weapons. "Who are you?" Both turned away because Riel's face was shining like the sun. He was very different from the boy they had entered Paradise with.

Both Uriel and Fammy looked at each other quizzically and then leaped back in defensive positions. Uriel was huge and had a distinctive hump behind his shoulders. Fammy had turned a tawny gold and black, but Uriel was the one to be reckoned with; he had doubled in size, huge rippling muscles below his shiny black and tan fur. There was a ring of gold fur around his collar which only emphasized his size. He was easily twice the height of Riel and ten times his weight. Suddenly all of them realized what had happened: Being in Paradise had changed them all; made them bigger, brighter, more than what they had been.

"Where do we go from here? Does anyone know?" inquired Mini.

"We head due south from here. I only know we need to free some people from something ahead. Look there are the supplies, packs and sleeping rolls under that tree over there. Liam warned me that you are not to be seen by humans until we unbind these people. This is especially true for you Mini; the Lord warned me that you would become a hat if you didn't take great caution. You know it's funny, but I can't seem to recall what happened in Heaven with any detail, it is all blurry, except for a few commands and where we need to go. Why are you all looking away from me?"

Mini replied, "What happened to you Riel? Your face is shining like the sun. None of us was ever understood by any man before you and we know how cruel they are towards all of us. There are few that are gentle and kind to us. Riel, none of us can bear looking at you!"

"Because we have been in Heaven, and with the Almighty, it is Liam's glory that is left over in my face," said Riel. "No one has been with Him and not been greater, more beautiful and changed after having seen Him. I can hardly believe we were there. You were all there too with me. You all look so different." While Riel replied he glanced down at his body. He had transformed from an adolescent into a man in a few short days. None of them were aware that what they perceived to be a few days in Paradise were, in fact, four years.

Riel went over to the pond and stood ankle deep in the water and then kneeled, looking at his reflection. His body was that of toned man.

The V-shape of his torso firm against a blue stretchy tunic. His long black hair wound with colored leather ties into a lengthy braid. The tendrils that escaped being bound curled around his handsome, sharply- featured face. It seems everything on his body was larger. Even in the water, he could hardly stand looking into his face as it was still bright with the shekinah glory. He went over to the packs and cut piece of cloth for a face shield with his knife, tied it around his face only leaving his eyes uncovered. Over the next few hours, the light in his face grew less and less as reality set in.

It didn't take long for them to make camp and start cooking dinner. Afterward Riel and Mini investigated the supplies that were left for them and found one of the packs had three sets of clothing for Riel. The first outfit made for travel was soft forest green and included tawny buckskin, knee-high boots with triple soles and designs decorated with tiny glass beads using gold thread. The second was the outfit he had on. The third was a priest's outfit worth the ransom of a king. It had a purple full-length robe finely embroidered with pomegranates and Lyons on the collar, hem, and sleeves; over it went an ephod of pure white linen set with twelve different gemstones attached to the inserted breast plate.

The three-quarter length sleeves were also embroidered with palm leaves, pomegranates, and cedar trees. The gemstones in the breast plate were separated into four rows of three. The first row contained a "Sardis (red carnelian or sard) sometimes known as a ruby, blue topaz, carbuncle (red garnet) and then a bright green emerald. The second row had sapphire, diamond, ligure (lapis lazuli), agate. The last row contained amethyst, beryl, onyx, and jasper."[1] A blood red cape completed the ensemble, the collar and sleeves trimmed with pure white ermine. The ephod had two large onyx stones with clips which held the shoulders to the garment. The shoes were emerald encrusted and made of woven gold. A miter (conical headdress) and a braided gold girdle for Riel's waist completed the outfit. The pack itself was plain and looked like all the other packs made of deerskin. Each of items had a special compartment in the pack.

As Riel inspected the clothing, the animals each took turns touching and looking at the jewels. "I think these stones mean something to you humans, don't they? They are so pretty! I especially like the bright green one and the shiny clear one," said Lawrence.

"Indeed, each stone has meaning, but many men have put their trust into wealth. I believe Liam has provided these garments not so that I claim riches, but my position. These are worth great sums of money and now we must be very careful to conceal them at every turn," replied Riel.

They set out the next morning but there was no great hurry, so they often discussed things between them, stopping at lakes and glades they liked, sometimes staying for a couple of days. It was a pleasant time for them. The days in Heaven were now almost completely faded for all of them, the only thing that

---

[1]   Exodus 39:10-13

reminded them was their physical appearance. A few weeks later, both Uriel and Fammy suddenly stopped on the path and started sniffing the air. "Riel, men have crossed through here some weeks ago with their horses, many of them too," said Uriel.

"I noticed," replied Riel. "I sense a difference in the road too. It is time for all of you to stay behind and be extremely careful to leave no sign, and to remain completely hidden until I return for you. However, I think, Mini, you can come with me and hide in my clothing or pack. You are just small enough to easily conceal and I have a feeling you will be most useful. The rest of you need to find a place closer to where I am going but make sure you can hide easily."

First Riel put on his forest green outfit and adjusted his backpack. Then he placed the costly priest garment pack back on Lawrence along with items he did not need. "You will have to help Lawrence get this off. However, together, I am sure you will figure out how to hide and HELP each other."

The next day, alone on the road, the track had widened. Riel sensed someone was tracking him. He proceeded over the lip of a hill and in the distance could see a pink cliff that had marks of habitation. He decided to stop under a tree and see what would happen.

Suddenly, a large man dressed in a green tunic cut to his thighs with matching tights, stepped out from a nearby tree. The man started to approach Riel who was sniggering under his breath. The man had a large yellow cap on, with a long bright pink feather attached. Riel had never seen anything like it. If he planned to hide in the forest with that, he'd have to make it invisible. It just looked ridiculous. Two more men jumped out and joined him and all three had different colored caps with colorful feathers in them. They looked like clowns.

"I am Riel Ran, son of the Silkies. I am wandering the earth in search of people who are different to learn and explore their culture." Riel extended his hand to the first man.

"You will come with us," said the first man to reach him, scowling and ignoring the outstretched hand. More well-armed men dressed like clowns appeared around him. Riel noticed they untucked their feathers from their shirts as they stepped out from the trees.

Riel did not reply but walked with the group towards the cliff castle after being searched and disarmed. The men searched his backpack and travel bags but did not find Mini even though she let out a strange squeak at one point. Riel acted like he did not hear it and the men were so consumed with searching they did not pay attention. Of course, they sneezed a lot since the feathers in their caps kept tickling each other's faces. Riel realized the brighter and longer the feather, the higher the rank so the first man to reveal himself was their leader. Riel looked at their serious faces and chuckled at the contrast between them and their rank feathers.

An hour later, an entourage had formed and followed the procession up a giant causeway to a set of intricately carved gates with tall columns that went up the entire height of the cliff. The causeway was a clever defense mechanism as the way switched back and forth as they climbed. The way was set with large pink pavers which were interlocked into a cross shape. The balustrades away from the cliff face were waist high, filigreed with designs of birds and forests. Along this barrier, posts with gold knobs were set every twenty feet. Benches were set into the other side with flowering vines and attractive tables carved literally into the walls. Two springs flowed from above creating waterfalls with pools at the junction where the road changed directions.

Lush trees and flower beds were planted right up to the gates above. It was so well-done Riel gasped when he realized the extent and quality of the workmanship. A large level terrace full of decorated planters finished the architecture at the gates. The view behind was breathtaking and so beautiful Riel exclaimed, "What a people you are to have designed and maintained this place of beauty. I've never seen anything like it." Just when he said this, a small flash of Paradise flew through his mind, but the memory was soon gone.

Riel walked with the men through the gates but before he entered, he noticed a small window high above and a little man who stuck his head out. It was only when the long pink feathered General signaled him that the three feet thick gates trembled and then swung open. Riel studied the design on the gates while they waited for the doors. The carved scene on them was of the very same valley they had just traversed with a huge Lyon roaring from the cliff palace on the left and distant mountains on the right.

The sun was setting on the whole scene. He wondered what that meant? He would ask if he got a chance.

They entered a huge cavern with several openings on the far wall. The ceiling was hundreds of feet above them and in places open to the sky. Giant beams crossed above with chandeliers hung with lanterns. Riel noticed dwarves running on the beams above. The room ended in a series of much smaller caves shooting off in all different directions. Halfway up the wall was a series of small cut windows. Even though the light was much lower, there were still planters and purple flowering trees at the edges. They led Riel though one of the openings then through a maze of tunnels cut right out of the rock.

From time to time a small window looked out on the valley below as they climbed and climbed higher in the castle. Finally, they entered a chamber that was twice the size of the one at the gates. It also had a set of entry doors which were wide open. The city inside was magnificent: the homes were of all different colors set on roads of the same pink cross pavers.

The streets went off radially every few degrees and the homes got larger with bigger lots and accommodations at the ends where the angles allowed more room. The middle lane was the widest and the one they took through the city.

The roof had openings to the sky high above but this time they used mirrors to increase the light below. Riel noticed that when it rained, buckets were rotated under the holes and they drained to a downward sloping channel and then further, to a cistern located to the left of the city. It looked like it was even larger than the city itself. These people were resourceful as well as clever. They eventually arrived at a set of smaller gates at the end of the middle pathway. These gates were shining solid gold again with the same design as the gates at the entry. They opened as they approached.

It opened into an ornately furnished room that held a single raised throne on a dais. A small man stepped out from behind the throne. He was covered in an ornate purple robe, a gold cap on his head adorned with a blue and turquoise peacock feather almost as big as he was.

Riel was surprised as the man's voice boomed when he spoke into the now crowded room.

The little King said, "Riel it is said you come from a far country. Do you intend harm? What is your mission among the Elegant?"

"I am a traveler and I have come to gather knowledge of peoples far and wide. I intend no harm to you or your people at this juncture," replied Riel in an equally booming voice. The room must have amplified the sound.

"Then enter our home and be welcome traveler," said the King.

The King signaled, and the room quickly emptied as four guards remained to accompany Riel onto the Dais. Curtains were drawn back and beyond a large entryway two fountains with carved stone Lyons had water spraying out of their mouths. The water gathered in a large deep pool and was set between a double set of curved stairwells to the left and right. The King went up the right staircase, entered a set of double doors into another very large chamber with columns and another raised throne. Riel followed with his guards who had never let their attention slip.

Riel was left standing twenty feet from the King. "Where do you come from? What clan do you belong to and why are you here stranger?"

"I am Riel Ran. I have no clan, but I was raised on a coastal island more than a thousand miles from here. I am gathering knowledge from those who walk the earth, learning of their ways and customs. I came to you as this is where my path led me."

"I am Kester the Supreme Leader and Holy Counselor to the Elegant. We welcome you to the Valley of Lights and will show you every courtesy. It has been many years since anyone has come in peace. Do not be fooled though! You will be monitored until we are assured of your intentions. Even if you are a spy, you will find our defenses formidable. No one can break them."

Two doors opened to the right side of the chamber and a dozen lovely women entered carrying trays with food on them. Another door opened and Kester came down off his throne, gesturing to another set of doors opposite where the women had entered. As Riel stepped through them, he gasped in wonder. A room opened onto the terrace he could see from the road; the roof was thirty feet above the dining area. The walls covered in flowering fuchsia vines, and the far area open to the terrace beyond. The terrace was just below the very cliff top and overlooked a panorama of everything below.

Riel was led to the table and seated to the King's right, some distance away with a guard stationed in between. Riel's mouth watered at the wafting smells from the dozens of savory dishes placed before them. He waited while Kester outlined several invisible runes in the air while chanting. Then King Kester began to pray.

"Oh, mighty King of the Universe, we exalt you to guide and protect the Elegant the most supreme and best of your peoples. We, your people, place our trust in your holy hands, as your name is higher than any other name. We seek your guidance as to our visitor Riel who has come to us in the name of peace. May we discern his true purpose in this.

"Protect us from the King in the Prophecy who would destroy the Elegant and our ways. Put your mantle of peace upon us as we rest in the shadow of your beauty, in this our home, the Citadel. Keep the Sloven in the earth below to keep our needs well met. Bless, this our meal to our good and to your purpose, we pray. Amen."

Riel was curious about some of the statements made in the prayer but waited to question the King about them. The meal was scrumptious. He asked Kester many questions about the Citadel and the Elegant. He learned that they were served by the Sloven, who were dwarves who lived in a cavern below the city. The King snarled every time he mentioned them and told Riel they were lower than dogs covered in fleas.

King Kester also questioned Riel about his travels. Riel left out the Dragon and, of course, never mentioned the animals he traveled with. Riel answered as best as he could without giving any prudent details, especially about his visit to Paradise.

Suddenly two trumpets sounded, and two doors that lead back to the throne room opened. A woman entered. Her dark hair was twisted into two braids coiled with pearls. Her tightly fitted midnight-blue gown revealed a tiny waist, high firm breasts and large hips. It was her face that froze Riel: A perfect oval set with two huge dark eyes, a tiny, upturned nose and two large red lips. Her stunning, exquisitely delicate face looked as if a light from Heaven illuminated it. In stunned silence, he could only stare at her as she entered, kissed her father's cheek, and sat down opposite him.

Kester turned to Riel and said, "This is my beautiful and only daughter, Astar." He then turned to her and said, "Pride of my life and beauty of the century, would you care to eat with us?"

Astar responded, "Yes Father I am hungry as the Sloven have done a terrible job on my face and hair today. I had to beat Lazarus and here comes the little pig thing now."

A man not more than three feet tall entered the room. His garment was covered from head to toe in combs, brushes, hair ornaments, various ointments, make-up containers, and gels, each of them looped onto his skintight red robe. He had a bright plume of mohawk styled blue hair, tiny pig-like green eyes, a huge nose with an upturned end, red freckled cheeks, but what dominated them all were the huge wing-like ears that took over his small head like two giant elephant ears.

Astar turned to Lazarus retrieving a multi-lash whip with metal ends from her belt and hit the little man's sensitive ears. He did not cry out, but two huge tears coursed down his face as he struggled to stay standing in front of her. Screaming into his face not two inches in front of her she said, "Next time I tell you to attend me, do not delay. And you just stay where I can lash you easily for your disobedience. You filthy, low animal and to think I was the one who brought you up from the dark caverns." Lazarus remained at attention in front of her.

Riel, struggling not to take the whip from her hand said, "What was his offense that you strike him?"

Astar's cheeks turned high with color, and she said, "Sloven were created by God to serve the Elegant. They are lowest of the Earth's living creatures. I found this filthy thing groveling in a coal cavern and I chose to bring him into our world of light. How does the snake repay me? He's disobedient, slow and an utter slob. I should never have brought him out, but I had to replace one of my six attendants and he was the least dirty of the lot." At that, she turned and struck him across his upturned face. Two more tears and a ribbon of bright blood formed above his left eye and dripped onto the floor. Still, he remained at attention.

Before she could use the whip again, Riel reached across the table and with a lightning movement grabbed it. Astar was so surprised she stared at her hand for a moment.

Riel said, "An interesting weapon indeed. The ornate carving on the handle is inlaid with silver. Where do the Sloven come from?"

Astar tried to retrieve the whip from Riel, but he was far too quick for her. She said, "The animals breed in their dens below the mountain where God does not shine on them. They are born without light or goodness. They are designed to serve our needs. I will have this one put out of his misery if you wish it. I know in your heart you want to be with me and have my beauty reflect onto you. I see it in your eyes."

"Ah," replied Riel, "If they are born without goodness, why is this one serving you?"

"He does not serve me; he attends me as God in Heaven has ordained," said Astar.

"Yet you would take his life and God has ordained he serve you?" asked Riel.

"God has given us dominion over the animals; To let them live or die and that is my right. Just as the cow or pig die to provide you with sustenance," replied Astar.

Riel noticed her red lips were curled in a surly, nasty look.

"They breed as animals do. Now there are many of them below," injected Kester. "My sweet, kind, and generous daughter has brought many of them up from the pit. She is so enlightened! It was her idea to have them attend her as we believed that they were not intelligent enough to fix hair or attend to our baths." He smiled at his daughter in obvious pride.

"Would you or the King miss this one if I was to have it attend me? I am curious to see what the thing can learn and do. If I am displeased, you can kill it." Riel attempted to put a surly look on his face. The Silkies would have laughed but Astar and Kester took him seriously.

Astar said, "Take the little beast then. I have always hated those ears of his and he is downright ugly, even for a Sloven."

Lazarus then moved to Riel's side of the table. Astar and King Kester continued their conversation discussing all kinds of things pertaining to the Kingdom they ruled. To make sure they thought he was listening, he would stop them and asked a few questions. He noticed the Sloven working around the room, cleaning, and serving him and the King and his daughter.

They took trays from the table and replaced them with fresh ripe fruit and a lovely nectar to drink.

Astar shivered as she carefully took a tiny fruit and placed it between her lips and teeth. She lowered her eyelids as she spoke, often stealing glances at Riel. He reacted by ignoring her completely. The blood had mostly dried on Lazarus's chin but a few more drops dripped onto the floor. He stood at attention beside Riel, his tiny eyes glistening with tears.

Riel stretched and let out a huge yawn.

"Oh, we are not being good hosts," cried Kester. He stood, walked across the room, picked up a mallet and hit a large gong. The doors sprung open and the women who served the food flooded into the room. He gave them instructions.

Riel was led down a long hallway with many doors. Finally, one of the women opened a door into a chamber which also had an open-air terrace. However, this was on the opposite side of the Citadel from the King's terrace and much smaller.

The late afternoon sun blazed into the room giving it a comforting glow. A huge bed dominated the whole affair although the bright colorful drapery that covered the walls screamed for attention too. Blue and Gold upholstered furniture stood in little groups about the chamber. It was elegant and a well-planned arrangement. One wall was mirrored with tiny glass squares from floor to ceiling reflecting the light from the open terrace.

A triangular fresco of blue hued tiles framed above the bed on the ceiling depicted a hunting scene in the valley below. It was intricate and so well done it looked like a painting.

Riel let out a huge sigh and yawned again. The women placed a tray of fruit and delectable deserts on the table near the entrance.

The left the room and closed the door leaving Lazarus in attendance.

No sooner had they left the room than Riel turned to Lazarus, "Are you okay? Is your eye alright?" Riel walked over to the sink at the far side of the room and returned with a wet cloth thinking to help Lazarus.

"Riel, you must never address me directly ever," said Lazarus. "Turn away as you speak and use anger in your voice. I will whisper instructions to you as I can. Act as though you cannot even see me. GO to the door and knock as they have locked you in. Ask for a singer and a glass of wine. Use that cloth to wipe your own brow and do not try to attend me or they will know what is going on."

Riel did exactly as Lazarus instructed. Soon a knock was heard two small Sloven women entered. The women's features were not as distorted or uneven as Lazarus's; they were a little taller and had long braided hair. One brought a bottle of wine and the other brought an instrument and a small, ladder which she stood on. She began to sing, and Riel turned in amazement; her voice was like no other, crystal notes rang out. Lazarus bumped into Riel's knee and indicated he wanted to speak, carefully indicating with his tiny hands that they needed to move to the chairs at the other end of the room. Riel, stretched and yawned again and he carefully and slowly made his way to the other end of the room near the open terrace, pretending to be interested in the decorations on the furniture.

They were all gold, and some were beautiful, but most were of animals mating. As Riel took a seat, Lazarus took a large bowl of spice scented water, removed Riel's boots, and began to wash and massage his feet. The singer moved her ladder to the sight line between the mirrored wall and where Riel was sitting. She began another song. Lazarus whispered, "Are you the King in the Prophecy?" Riel realized that the mirrored wall was a front for spying. It would be difficult to spot an eye watching in the complicated maze of tiles.

Lazarus continued to wash Riel's feet; his head bent. He again whispered, "Is this the beginning of our freedom? There is an old painting on a side entry below. It shows you with a pair of Filk bears, a Donkey that's black and white and a Marmot. It sure looks like you."

Riel whispered back by pretending to drink his wine, "I am not certain although the painting you describe is convincing."

Lazarus whispered, "I am Lazarus as you know, but I am the leader of the Sloven. It was predicted at my birth you would be coming, and I would be the one to lead my people to freedom. We do not have long to talk today as soon the bells will sound and I will have to return below. But tomorrow they have the mathematicians working down below this very room. We are doing the computing but two of Kester's 'High Ones Enlightened' or HOE take credit and act like they know what they are talking about. It takes ten of our finest minds to calculate what they are planning. Ask if you can speak to the HOE.

"Kester will be so proud to show you how they have calculated the orbit of the moon and the predictions for the future phases. Stop to beat me a few times but make your blows to these padded areas on my body inside my clothing. We have long awaited you. Many were killed recently as the Elegant culled our numbers. I was spared to do Astar's hair and serve her. But I hear my children's and wife's screams every time I try to sleep. Tonight, I need you to leave the whip in this very chair. We will have one of our spies come in and replace the metal tips with soft pliable material. I will cry out and grovel in front of you, take no mercy.

"Do not hit my ears though, they are particularly sensitive and Astar knows that, and it is why she hits me there." Suddenly, the bell sounded. The singing stopped and the Sloven were gone an instant later.

Riel's backpack was on a chair by the door. He retrieved it and put it on the bed unpacking the contents. The bottom was cleverly designed to hold Mini complete with a flap so she could see complete with air holes.

No one could see it was there unless they knew about it.

Riel whispered, "Mini are you there?"

A tiny voice said, "I am, Riel! But it is hot in here and I am very tired. They almost found me this afternoon and I was very scared."

"They have manhandled this pack several times today and they thoroughly searched everything you have in here. I am so glad I am so well concealed. Who was the dwarf you were talking to?"

Riel looked and saw one of the mirrored tiles move and an eye appear. "We are being closely watched Mini. I will have to wait until it is dark to talk to you. You can hide under the bed when I put the pack on the floor. Use the small flap on the bottom and get out of there." Riel put the pack on the floor. Mini scrambled out underneath the bed.

Riel went into the bath area which also had its own small terrace. The huge blue tiled tub already had hot steaming water with floating rose petals.

To the side of the bath's marble shelf, small alabaster jars held almost priceless pungent bath oils from far lands.

Another male Sloven stood in the corner in attendance. He held an armload of thick cotton towels. "I am allowed to stay in your attendance until the second bell sir," the tiny man said. "The King gave me dispensation to stay but I must leave shortly. My name is Joshua, and I am your servant." Then he whispered, "Is it true?"

Riel threw the man a cautious look. "What would I need a useless creature such as you to give me a bath! Yes, it is true that I would beat you if I had my whip. Now leave before I throw you off the terrace myself."

Joshua bowed from his waist, set the towels next to the tub and left. "As you desire my Master." The second bell sounded.

In the night, Mini had got up on the bed and hid underneath the large pillow Riel's head was resting on. She touched Riel's ear. "What is going on?"

Riel took a few moments to reply whispering into his pillow like he was in a dream.

He soon found out that Mini had talked to a couple of the Sloven who were hidden in the vine just outside on the terrace. The Cliff Castle was apparently honeycombed with secret passages leading up from the caverns below. Only the Sloven knew about them and used them to their advantage when they could. Only the King's quarters were not connected to the rest of the chains leading up the Cliff Castle, as the king was extremely well guarded. They had to run across some open hallways that were also well guarded. A few weeks before, the Sloven were surprised by a raid on their homes in the caverns and many died. At that turn, they permanently stationed people who spent hours inside the KIng's quarters in tightly enclosed spaces. Because of this, Mini found Sloven hiding in the vine getting fresh air during the night.

The next morning Riel found the whip back on the chair. The tips were indeed soft and pliable but looked like metal.

King Kester lived at the topmost layer of the Castle and above Riel's room ceiling, centurions patrolled, and archers stood at ready. During the night, Mini explored and overheard the King talking with one of the captains. Apparently, they liked the abuse Riel was giving the Sloven. They thought Riel might work out to be a worthwhile ally because Astar was at a marriageable age, and she was strongly attracted to Riel. Kester believed that Riel was much more than a traveler but held rank and position where he came from. Riel could work out to be a valuable pawn as Astar was well trained from an early age as a seductress. If that failed, they would use the pheromones from the wizard's collection. He would talk with his daughter and instruct her not to continue the clandestine visits from her lovers now that Riel was available. One thing bothered him though, where was Riel's entourage as true kings and nobles never traveled by themselves?

Riel saw Astar at breakfast. Mini had determined that a visit to the cavern was in order. She had hidden inside Riel's robe. Riel put tiny pieces of food into his pocket that soon disappeared. Astar was in a good mood, entering the breakfast hall swirling in a blue silk gown. She was beyond lovely in the morning light as she swayed slowly, provocatively towards the table. Pearls dripped over her brow and a large ruby rested on her forehead.

Her eyes sparkled with delight when she connected with Riel's eyes from halfway across the room. Riel could not take his eyes from her: she was like a dancing deer crossing a lush meadow. However, in a sudden flash of spiritual insight, he saw a vision of her in darkness like a swaying snake. Over her head, a vortex of swirling black clouds formed and in them were three small children's faces, one of them a baby. He knew she was the mother of three children already! Then the vision was gone.

Astar sat at the table. He shuddered at the darkness of it. What had happened to her children? Riel's heart cried within him for her beauty and her terrible ugliness. He blinked a couple of times as tears formed in his eyes.

King Kester thought Riel was crying in adoration of his daughter, and the thought of it brought tears to his eyes. He beheld Astar's beautiful face, highly colored with lust for Riel. His plan would succeed if he could manipulate Riel into marrying her. First though, he needed to find out who exactly Riel really was. He walked and acted like a king or nobleman, he thought like them, and he reacted like one too. Who was this man? Kester sent out emissaries to every corner of the Western Kingdom.

Riel looked at Kester and wondered why he had teary eyes too, but he said, "I am curious about your Mathematicians. I have heard of great men plotting the stars and moon, but you said you had a group of them working today. I would like to see and understand what you are doing and maybe understand the logic behind the calculations. I marvel at your cleverness as a people. My room is more than pleasant, but that bath is just incredible. How did you get water to and from the bath so high up in the cliff? How did it remain hot while I bathed? You are indeed an incredible people, wondrous even."

The King ate every compliment with a growing sense of appreciation. Kester smiled as he considered his brewing devious plans. "Perhaps you would like to visit the room where we do our calculations? It has a moving ceiling."

Riel kept his face straight as he agreed to visit the Mathematicians below. Astar was sitting across from Riel her face flushed with warm desire, her shapely legs visible beneath the see-through cover of her dress, her made-up eyes glued to Riel's. She smiled at him, hoping like her father that she would soon be able to put another notch in her belt and take her time exploring his fine body. Her desire grew as she let her eyes drift down his magnificent torso.

Kester and Riel stood and left the room, leaving Astar not invited. No matter to her, she had a new Sloven, and she hoped to get her beautiful hair in a particularly attractive coif for this evening because Astar and her father had decided to throw a dinner in honor of Riel's visit. She needed a bath in costly oil and perfume and then wanted to see which outfit would be most attractive. It would take the whole afternoon. She fingered her new whip which was a little longer and had barbed metal tips at the crops multi-lash end. Riel had kept the old one from the night before. Thinking about that, her anticipation grew as she thought about making her new Sloven cry out when she struck her ugly body. Maybe this new Sloven was really a Godsend? Lazarus was particularly immune but often had tears in his eyes and that was no fun.

Kester and Riel found out that the Mathematicians had moved into the Sloven's cavern when they arrived at the room below. It took them the better part of an hour to achieve the main gates. They turned at the main gate and a secret door opened to their left just as they arrived. This opened into a small cavern which had a large wooden undecorated door at the far end. Kester took a huge key from the attendant and fitted it into the locking mechanism. Sounds of turning gears and grinding metal ensued and the gate opened a tiny bit. The attendants opened it further.

A second smaller door was ahead and the whole ritual was done again except this door took two keys which had to be twisted in tandem. The next door was huge, at least twelve feet across and had an arch at the top. Five men abreast could walk through it easily. Three keys had to be turned in this one at the same time and it sprung open. A dark hallway lit by torches led down inside the mountain. The guards handed Kester and Riel torches from the barrels inside this gate.

Then they lit them. Then five of the King's personal guard went ahead leading the way. They were well armed and had their swords at ready. Down, down, down they went as the temperature dropped. Small anterooms began to appear and soon ten Sloven were trailing behind the King's entourage. There were five more of the King's guard to the rear and they kept a close watch on the Sloven. The hall turned back on itself.

As they turned the bend a huge lengthy painting dominated the further wall.

Someone had tried to chisel off the rock face in places to desecrate the piece.

Several torches lit the rest of the depicted scene. All the men were Sloven in the painting except for obviously added poorly rendered stick figures. As they walked down, the painting got less and less desecrated and soon it was whole. It went on for hundreds of feet, it must have taken a century to paint.

Riel stopped to admire the work from time to time but had to double time to keep in front of the rear guard. Riel realized it was the story of the Sloven from creation on. Liam appeared from time to time but he was a Sloven with Liam's features. He noticed the stick figures stopped about halfway down. At first, the Sloven appeared as a free people but then three Elegant appeared on huge black war horses.

There was a massacre and the remnant Sloven were carried off to Cliff Castle as slaves. The Elegant destroyed their homes and crops as they left leaving a scorched earth behind. Then one whole ten-foot painting section was missing. Three Sloven in fifty rags were busy removing it with hammers and chisels. Their faces showed the strain of doing a job they abhorred but when Riel walked by, they started whispering to each other. Riel connected his eyes with one of them and secretly motioned for them to stop looking at him.

The captain of the guard said, "We have yet to find out who is painting the walls back King Kester. The dirty, destitute little dogs are getting the paint from somewhere and they manage to repaint it before we return in the mornings. How many of them have we sent to their deaths to stop this travesty? I am going to assign more of the Sloven on the hammer and chisel crew when we return topside."

"Do not do that," replied the King. "Since we have culled the herd, they are not making the same quality mini cakes or icing. I do love those. And others have noticed they are having to beat the animals more often. Let it rest and see if things improve. If not, we will send another group of their children off the cliff." The King shook his head in disgust.

The captain said, "You know I cannot fathom how they manage to increase their numbers the way they live down here. They are like rats in a barrel. But I will have them watched more closely now and I will personally observe the bakery myself."

Before Riel thought about it, he said, "If the paintings reappear why don't you hang curtains over the pieces you don't like and re-assign the Sloven to the bakery?" He was sorry he had said anything but now he would be much more circumspect.

The captain replied, "You have no idea what we put up with: Their animal minds cannot conceive a single elegant thought. The curtains would be left on the floor in the morning, and we'd have to kill more of them to stop that. They have become lazy, and we are not getting the services we deserve as their masters." All the Elegant entourage nodded their heads vigorously at once.

The painting became systemically darker spiritually and physically as they walked on, ending with horrific scenes of slaughtered and degraded Sloven children laying at the bottom of the Cliff Castle. It was affecting Riel and he was trying not to react and give himself away.

Then up ahead, a light and a large hall. On the far wall a single large 20 by 30-foot painting dominated. There he recognized himself with all his animal friends standing on a cliff looking back at the Cliff Castle. But he had on the Elegant's clothes and one of their ridiculous feathered hats. Fortunately, in the painting, he was turned away and his face was not visible, but he'd be known if anyone recognized his conspicuous decorated boots but only a portion of them were visible. He would hide the real ones when he got back to the room and hope that none of them noticed when they searched his pack. The scene showed the well-armed Elegant standing by the Windrift River. Riel was facing them with the animals.

There were a few half-hearted stick figures painted over the top, but it was obvious they did not belong. One of them covered over parts of the boots so they were not as prevalent as they should have been.

They continued through one of three large doorways. Noises of habitation could be heard in the darkness up ahead, but the King turned to a wood door in the left tunnel. They walked in but all of them were momentarily blinded: Two wide stone ceilings opened 45 feet above allowing sunshine to slant into the wide well decorated and equipped room.

When Riel's vision was cleared, he could see two people standing beside gold thrones with a tall table between them busy drawing on sheets paper. The other end of the room was for calculations with several Sloven sitting at small desks. The middle was dominated by several Sloven scribes.

The Mathematicians began bickering, but one stopped and noticed the King and his group of visitors.

They turned in attendance. Riel saw they both were well supplied with wine and a tray of tasty treats on their drawing table. Behind them was another huge painting of the midnight sky and a rendition of the Citadel. Two gold curtains framed the painting. It was a comfortable and nice place to work.

King Kester said, "How goes it Etharis and Elgenius?"

Both had a haughty look on their pale faces, but Etharis answered, "We have pronounced the world to be round and we have calculated the Moon's phases accurately.

"Come look at our designs!"

The King stepped forward and studied their drawings and calculations. Riel noted they were crudely drawn, and it was not clear what the orbits were. However, when he looked at that the drawings the Sloven were working nearby, he noted they were technical and rendered in precise ovals. Riel thought that it was not the Elegant who were calculating anything.

"Work well done from two of most intelligent Elegant, Riel. Meet, Riel a visitor who has come from the Western Sea a thousand miles from here. He gives us hope that one day others my come to visit and see what our people have to offer." The King smiled at Riel.

The two gave a slight bow and greeted him with a look of disdain. Riel looked shabby in comparison with their bright purple caps, hot pink long feathers and embroidered robes covered in mathematical equations. They men were short for Elegant, but it was their stout bodies that filled in the tight robes they wore that tickled Riel. He smiled and bowed too. He almost laughed but held it in trying to discern if these two could calculate anything. He asked a few elementary questions from basic Algebra but noted the men had to consult a tiny smart-looking Sloven to get the answer. The two Elegant retrieved several charts from a cupboard nearby.

The King and the guards started discussing the charts with the mathematicians and Riel feigned like he did not understand. He stood back at the edge of the circle beside the tiny intelligent looking Sloven man.

Riel whispered, "Did you design this room?" Riel pointed at the retractable ceiling. "No, I did not. It was my great, great, great grandfather. He did wondrous mechanical things in his time."

"Remember me? My name is Joshua, and I gave you the bath towels. I redid the tips on your whip. You need to use it when Lazarus joins us shortly. They are getting skeptical, and this is not good. We have put pints of animal blood in his clothes that will open when you hit him. Do not worry, it is all for show. If you listen closely, you can hear Lazarus laughing below in anticipation. It is funny that you are asking them elementary equations with the Math-might-miss-them."

Riel laughed. However, the Elegant did not notice so he continued by saying, "Why have you endured so much Joshua? These people are very mean-spirited towards you."

"We have been here almost 400 years. We have tried many times to leave but we must bring our children and the elderly. There are many more Sloven below that the Elegant do not know about. We cannot get out of the Citadel without being sighted by the guards. You can't move 3,000 people without leaving a trail. Besides the Prophecy told of a single man coming who was a King. He will find a way when there was no way.

"The Elegant kill us and destroy our children like we are vermin, yet we do all the work and serve them far beyond what we should. Below and beside this cavern, there is an up-side-down wedding cake hive built right down into the ground that the Elegant do not even know about with exits through this very room then up through the ceiling. We removed the soil we excavated when we built the ramp into the citadel four hundred years ago. They did not even notice or asked where all that material came from. We were much fewer and so were they.

"Elegant never come down here after the bells. We have hidden many Sloven but they only ones they see are the same ones. There are hidden passages everywhere in the Castle and many here below too. We disappear and can be hidden for months if we wish. But we need food and supplies and so we husband their farms and fields sneaking extra in at night. The Elegant sometimes have incredible perception and eyesight but they believe we are below the animals and so have missed their target. They have become lazy and fat and arrogant. All they do is guard us and beat us. King Kester and his vicious daughter are the most despicable we have had in many years. They murdered many of us a few months ago and my own Father was one of them. Lazarus lost his wife and two young children.

"When they did that, we knew that Prophecy had started and so we prepared, and we are physically and emotionally ready to leave this place behind and find a new life. We also noticed your boots at your arrival and covered them with the stick figures on the painting. They did not even notice your boots, but they will if you don't get meaner towards us and beat Lazarus in front of them."

Riel was amazed to have this much information passed, but the Elegant were still deep in discussion at the table. He said, "How am I to help you if I am only a single man?" At this Mini, hidden in a deep pocket let out a squawk. Riel put his fingers inside the pocket and rubbed her forehead which served to soothe her.

"I need to give you Mini, Joshua. She is here inside my jacket. Be very careful to peek inside when I open it to let you look. Joshua looked in and saw a smiling marmot, cozy in her small pocket nest. Be extremely careful that none of Elegant see you removing her.

"She is very precious to all of us, but I think you need to consult with her. When you are satisfied return her to the top of the Citadel. I am going to bend down and stretch. I will turn towards you, grab her as quickly as possible." In a swift movement, Mini was exchanged and Joshua backed out of the room bowing every few feet.

"As a distraction Riel said in a loud voice, "Does no one hunger? Cannot we adjourn to the light above my King?"

Lazarus had entered when Joshua left.

Etharus said to Riel, "you are below ground but we have prepared a feast back at the Lyon's gate. It should only take a few minutes to walk back up."

Riel turned to the door and pretended to stumble on Lazarus. He took the whip and hit him half-heartedly until he realized how well-padded Lazarus was and Lazarus had managed to give a brief grin and egg him on secretly. He went forward and blood spurted from various places on the garment. There was blood on the floor and Lazarus was writhing on the ground putting on a show worthy of an award. Riel really got into it too. Lazarus's face was covered in welts and blood, but Riel never hit him there even once: Only on the well-padded blood wet areas of his clothing. Two of the Elegant moved forward and kicked Lazarus, who was in a fetal position with his head and ears covered with his hands. Fortunately, they also hit padded areas, but Lazarus let out some mournful groans.

The Elegant started shouted, "Keep going! Kill the moron for making you stumble, there are more to replace him. Leave him here to die!"

Riel knew he had to get them out of there before they discovered the ruse. So, he said, "Now see you've got blood on my clothing, you horrible little pig and I am even more hungry from this beating. Can we please get something to eat and drink before I faint?"

The whole group left the room except for the Sloven and headed up the hall. Lazarus was left on the floor in a puddle of blood. He was still bruised in places and would be stiff and sore when we woke the next morning. But most of it was superficial except where the two Elegant kicked him on the ground. The padding helped but one rib was broken. The other Sloven rushed to help him up and carried him to the medical room below.

The Elegant were patting Riel on his back when he exited to the light above.

The gate terrace was set with tables, chairs and bunting with colored flowers. Colorful banners and flags flapped in the cool afternoon breeze. Delicious Hors d'oeuvres and hot and cold food awaited. Riel sat down and grinned and smiled as everyone greeted and smiled at him for beating the Sloven. Two beautiful women brought him his food and drink.

Riel retired and had a nice bath later that afternoon. The Sloven bath attendant whispered how pleased they were with the ruse, but Lazarus had received a broken rib in the process. He would be fine but now Riel would be accepted as one of the Elegant's own. He also included that a party was to be thrown in Riel's honor and Astar would be her most provocative.

Riel inquired in a low tone, "but I saw three children in my vision! What was that?"

The Sloven whispered, "She has already conceived three times, the first she had murdered at birth, the second two were sold to a passing slave trader. They were all from different men too. We tried to save them, but we failed." He hung his head.

Riel found a red expensive tunic with matching tights on his bed. The hat was atrocious with a bright green feather and the socks were so silly looking he burst out laughing.

The Sloven stood beside him and whispered again, "Pretend I told you a joke.

"Quickly, they have three people watching this room and they get deeply insulted about clothing."

Riel said, "that actually was funny told from an animal's point of view." He guffawed again.

He rested and relaxed the next hours and then got dressed when he woke. The Grand Hall was set with such beauty and elegance that Riel literally stopped in his tracks and stared when he entered. Purple dominated everything, and crystals were used with every light source. The effect was so beautiful and so alluring he almost forgot where he was and what was really going on. He imagined many Sloven had worked all day, to create this magnificence but would not get any credit and probably got beaten on top of it.

Every single Elegant was dressed in their finest, which meant mostly tights, feathers, and highly colored garments. They were milling about the food tables when Riel arrived. Riel noted that when he entered all he could see were heads of hued feathers like a whole flock of over-colored peacocks or turkeys. He smiled at that thought and walked into the crowd. On the terrace above a Sloven orchestra softly played music. He stopped at the ovens cooking hot bread. A Sloven woman handed him a piece of fresh) of hot bread soaked in herbed butter, along with a plate covered in hot tasty vegetables in different sauces and some fresh fruit. Then he went to the table where he sampled an assortment of shredded meats and even more tasty gourmet sauces. There was no use wasting all the Sloven labor. Even with all their mistreatment they always did their best.

After the sumptuous dinner the Elegant began to dance to the rhythmic upbeat music. Soft shaded light was hitting the grand hall from the last vestiges of sunlight so now all the candles and lanterns were lit. Riel paused to think about the cost in man hours for the design, labor, and supplies for assembling so many in one place. He physically cringed. As the meal ended trumpets were sounded, the hall was hushed as the doors burst open and Astar was carried in on a ruby encrusted throne lifted by six Sloven. Her hair was wound into braids on the top of her head, but many curls had escaped containment and the result was most becoming. Her dress was deep red the bodice covered in tiny seed diamonds. A circlet of gold with a large dripping pearl focused all eyes on her beautiful, stunning face. She had a rod set with gems in her hand. She set her face to Riel in the crowd and commanded the Sloven carrying her to him. When she arrived, she stood, swirled her cape, and bowed to Riel.

Riel reached for Astar's hand and said, "Do not bow." His head swam for a moment as he realized how different she appeared to what her spirt revealed. He was almost taken with her and without warning would have been lost. Then he remembered her hitting Lazarus and his face hardened. He dropped her hand.

She looked up at him and smiled but was confused when his face hardened, and he dropped her hand. Just then one of the servants dropped a priceless colored crystal bowl full of fruit. It shattered right in front of Riel and the little woman dropped to the ground as an Elegant man began to strike her. Riel heard his name whispered behind him. He leaned down to hear, "She has a perfume on that bewitches men, do not allow her to touch your face or allow her to stand close to you or tomorrow you will wake in her bed committed. Take good care Riel, her beauty is already an enchantment."

Riel stood up and acted as though something had bitten his leg. He looked up and Astar was looking right into his face. She stepped close to him looking at him with such love and innocence, it became difficult to pull back when he got a whiff of her rapturous perfume. His head became fuzzy and he almost succumbed, but the same whisperer stepped on his toe, and he let out a tiny yelp. Astar was so dangerous and insidiously evil.

He turned his back to her and drifted into the crowd. He found King Kester at the other end of the hall on his throne.

The King motioned for Riel to approach. Riel took a seat at his knees and settled his back against the throne leg looking up into Kester's fine face. Riel thought about how well structured the Elegant's faces were. Most of them would be considered beautiful by any standard.

Riel said, "What are your thoughts oh worthy one?" Riel knew how to enchant too.

Kester replied, "My daughter is lonely and forlorn. No one has come forward in marriage, but she will not allow her body to be used unless it is in the bed of a worthy man whom she loves. She has cared for no one despite her great beauty and chastity. She is as pure as the winter snow and as beautiful as a falling star."

The lies dripped from his lips as he looked with sincerity into Riel's eyes.

Riel felt anger rise in his chest. Who were these people that enslaved others and used perfumes and deception to get what they wanted? He stopped himself from following that line of thought and realized he had not spent any length of time praying since he had arrived. The Lord would sort this all out, but he just needed time to listen one on one. Astar spent the rest of the night hunting for Riel, and he spent the night avoiding her. He greeted and charmed a number of Elegant maidens in retaliation before he left just to irritate her. He left early for his room; the prospect of prayer time lay upon his heart.

He practically ran up the last few corridors and took a quick bath and went to bed. He no sooner got settled when Joshua walked in the door. He stopped in his tracks when he realized Riel was already in bed.

"What are you doing Master?"

"I doubt if anyone is listening, my little friend, they were in middle of revelry when I left," said Riel. "Turn to your own home and family. I am peaceably settled and ready to pray."

Joshua looked around in fright, his eyes darted to the mirrored tiles. "Riel, it is better to be prepared and believe that our adversary is waiting for any slip. They may not punish you but my life and that of my family is on the line. Never again speak to me as a friend until the day you free us. You need to use your whip more often and speak harshly with any of us you encounter."

Just then a soft click was heard in the wall and an eye appeared behind the center tile. Joshua darted his eyes to Riel and back to the wall giving notice they were being watched again.

Riel said, "Get out of my sight you little pig. I expected you to attend me, but you were nowhere to be seen. If I was not in bed, I would beat you." Joshua ran from the room feigning fright. It was impressive.

Riel began to pray in silence but soon he was speaking in a hushed voice as the Holy Spirit swept over his soul filling him with sweet peace and assurance. He started praying for those he had met in the last few days but spent more time bringing up King Kester and especially Astar. They were his mortal enemies. God was always full of grace and Liam especially exhibited it. It was a long time for Riel fell asleep, but he awoke refreshed and set on a plan. He would wait until Mini returned with her report and keep up his charade until he knew what to do. It was never good to rush into things without adequate prayer and planning.

Kester was very out of sorts at breakfast. When Riel entered smiling, he scowled and said, "Where were you last night. And why are you mulling to yourself in bed?"

"I am praying for you and your people King Kester. After listening to you last night, I knew I needed some alone time," said Riel.

A nasty look crossed Kester's face. "YOU avoided my daughter who is more beautiful than the night sky. Why?"

"Her beauty is more breath taking than a sunset sky too, King Kester. I am not a man to rush into anything without first taking my time and making sure that things are on my terms and conditions. I cannot control my feelings in her presence, especially with the way she looked last night so I avoided the contact. That is what I must do for now."

"What about my daughter's feelings and needs?"

"She is an intelligent woman fully capable of controlling herself and those around her."

Now the King was truly perturbed. "She will never control me."

"That is obvious. You are and always will be in control of this Citadel," replied Riel.

12

PLANS MATURE

*"He that saith he abideth in him ought himself
also to walk even as he walked."*
1 John 2:6

O ver the next few weeks, Riel accompanied Kester on many little diversions.

Whenever Astar appeared, Riel left as soon as possible without insulting anyone. She tried many times to get physically close to Riel but never managed more than about three feet. It grew to be a contest of skill between them as she grew more and more determined to corner him. He was the very first to resist her. Her coy ploys grew into skilled warfare as meetings were set up in small dark places. They never took place because Riel saw right through her cunning and deception. He always stood ready, taking a different route to and from anywhere and making sure his terrace room was checked by Joshua before he entered. He made a point of being in the company of others if he chanced to meet her. If Riel was not with King Kester, he made plans with Etharis and Egenius who were often calling for him as they enjoyed his wit and company. Riel acted as though one girl had caught his interest.

He accepted an invitation to visit her family one afternoon but King Kester had called him to the throne room instead.

The King was in surly mood when Riel appeared before him. "It has come to my knowledge that the daughter of Elan, Elene has piqued your interest, Riel." Astar stood beside the throne a picture of misery: Her stunning face flushed and her eyes red with crying. Wispy curls escaped around her face but her long, silky auburn hair was free down her back. Riel looked at her and felt some longing. He wanted her soul to match her beauty.

"It is good for a man to have choice," replied Riel.

The King cringed and in a loud voice said, "Is it a prudent choice to want a rock when a diamond is available?"

"I have told you in our talks that I must have no ties until I finish my wanderings and return to my home country." Riel answered.

Astar whimpered and put her hand to her lips.

"So, this visit to Elene's family means what?" the King asked.

"King Kester, I took you for a man of discretion and I have modeled my behavior after you," said Riel. "I have visited many families here in your Citadel and we have dined at many women's tables. I thought I was complimenting you and your people by getting to know them. My time is limited here, and I want to know you and the ways you do things. Your people are smart and intelligent. I want to learn as much as I can to help my own people."

"But you avoid my own daughter at every turn! Why?"

"Her beauty is to be taken in tiny sips," said Riel. "I do not want to become intoxicated by her and say and do things I have no intention of fulfilling. I take her chastity as a great value to her and your Kingdom. I will not compromise my belief in her and you." At this, Astar wiped a huge tear rolling down her face. Her long dark lashes were wet and her eyes glistening with desire. It was hard for Riel to look away.

The King, looking at his distraught daughter shouted, "Riel I am going to ask you a direct question and you must answer me!"

"I have been known to fish," said Riel.

"Did you say fish? Don't even suggest that you are a fisherman," said the King. "I will never believe that. Look at the way you walk and the way your mind works! I never know if you are making fun of us or complimenting us. And the way you treat Astar: She has the beauty of a Queen and the heart of a Lyon. Yet you choose to spend your time with a common woman like Elene. You ignore and hurt Astar."

"Your inquiry did not include what I am fishing for," Riel exclaimed.

"What is it you fish for then?" said Kester.

"Men, King Kester. I want to know who they really are and what makes them do the things they do. I want to understand so I make better decisions and give my people wisdom when I return to them. I cannot be tied to anyone right now."

"Do your people consider you a leader?" Kester asked.

"Not at this time," Riel replied.

"Why do you not speak of them? Will they one day call you leader?" Kester asked.

"I do not speak of them because I do not understand them. They have a man in control who murders and maims even his own wife and children. I am only one man, but my heart grieves for the world's wrongs. I grieve for those who use deception and drugs to control and manipulate others." Riel looked directly into Astar's eyes when he said this. Her cheeks colored and she looked down.

The rest of the conversation revealed nothing to Kester, and he dismissed Astar and Riel both in consternation. Later that afternoon Astar called a meeting with General Enginele and her father.

Astar started the conversation between them in a very small anteroom to the throne room. They were all sitting at a high table. "I tell you; Riel knows. He has seen something or heard something about me and my past. I saw it in his eyes. I tell you both something is wrong here. That man is up to something."

The General said, "He has beaten the Sloven with the whip he took from your hand. He has never shown you any interest or reacted to your advances. Does that make him your enemy my Princess?"

"Not an enemy exactly but I tell you something is just not right. I can feel it," she replied.

The King looked at the General. "Has he said or done anything when he is alone with his servants or to indicate something is amiss?"

"He spends long hours tossing and turning in his bed mumbling. He sometimes wakes and goes out to the terrace at night still speaking in low tones like he is praying. But he is cruel to the Sloven and even crueler than some of us.

"Remember the beating he gave Lazarus right in front of us? Lazarus almost died and is just now only able to do a few of his duties and Riel would not let him come back to serve him. The man hates the little pigs. It is only your daughter he totally ignores, and she has never been ignored in her entire life." A sly smile slipped over his lips as he looked Astar up and down. Her reputation at the Guard was well founded.

"I tell you two that man knows something about me and something is going on here," said Astar. "I can see it and I know it."

"My daughter has told me many things about others that have all come true," said the King. "She is perceptive. We will double the watch and always keep Riel under surveillance. Astar, you leave the man alone for the next few weeks, perchance absence will make his heart grow fonder. He has looked at you daughter, I have seen it. You are right, something just does not add up here. He speaks very little of his home and I have never heard him speak of his family. He has only mentioned a sea and an island, but he walks, talks, and speaks like a king. His countenance takes on a certain strange glow from time to time and look at his fine face. He has the bearing, I tell you. We will find out what is going on here."

Riel heard a squeak underneath his bed when he walked into his room that evening. He could hardly wait to talk with Mini. He went out onto the terrace and looked out onto the valley. Cows were lowing in the meadow, trees were laden with fruit, lush fields of grain stretched to the horizon. It was refreshing to have it briefly rain in the afternoons from the thunderclouds forming above the distant mountains. Riel could smell lavender, the very last of the season growing in large clay pots on his terrace. What a lovely place this was. He began his evening prayers, bowing his head.

Later that evening Riel could feel the warm furry body of Mini next to him under the covers. "My friend I have missed you these past weeks. I have much to tell you Riel. First however, I will tell you of the conversation I overheard with the General and King regarding Astar." Riel thought after he heard Mini's story, *Well they think they have spies, little do they know what we have.*

The last weeks of summer were glorious. It was the mildest summer according to the Elegant's records and the store houses were full to bursting. Riel had found a way to speak to Lazarus. Lazarus came through the hidden passages inside the Citadel and exited one floor below Riel's room. Waiting until dark, he then climbed up the vine to Riel's terrace. The vine was so thick that Lazarus inserted a seat in a group of thick leaves where the boughs would bear his weight. He was not visible even in the daytime. Riel could clearly hear him even when he whispered, and Riel was standing out in the open thirty feet from any interior wall. The spies could only hear Riel mumbling and he did that a lot normally. Riel would cast a small stone off the terrace and watch it fall signaling Lazarus that the coast was clear. The stone clattered down the cliff landing on the terrace below.

"What a stunning evening," exclaimed Riel when he heard Lazarus get into his bough seat.

"You are going to have to quell a coming storm, Riel," said Lazarus. "It has been hard keeping secrets from the Elegant. They are perceptive if lazy. Elene, the girl you used to make Astar jealous has overheard some Sloven conversation. Fortunately, I think the mention of the word 'freedom' has been covered over. However, Elene is thinking you mean to marry her in the Spring."

Astar will hear that rumor soon and you can bet there is going to be an uproar.

"How can a place have such beautiful women, and yet they are depraved, even convincing themselves of their own lies," answered Riel. "I am sick of them all. Their Church services are so long, tedious, full of praises for themselves as God's elect. Yet they walk out and mistreat you, murder your children. They believe you are lower than animals, yet it is you who sustains and helps them. Lazarus, you are smart, clever, and wily. You remind me of Lawrence and Mini as they always have something to say." Riel missed his animal friends.

Lazarus, well settled into his comfortable nest, took out his pipe and lit it up. He was smiling with pleasure at Riel. He had fooled all the Elegant. Since his cave beating, the Elegant believed that Riel hated the Sloven. They thought he was even crueler than most of them. This was the biggest barrier preventing the Elegant from seeing what was really going on. The flowing animal blood released as he beat Lazarus convinced them. That had happened in early summer just after Riel arrived. Lazarus had laughed for weeks afterward. So now, because he was free from Astar, he had spent the whole summer preparing his people to move and be free. In thirty days, the night sky would be filled with a blazing comet. According to the Prophecy, when it appeared the Sloven would be freed from their imprisonment. Already, the storehouses were prepared with food and traveling wares. Mini had no small hand or paw in accomplishing this over the summer.

Lazarus let out a puff of smoke from his well-used pipe. "Well Riel what do I tell my people? ARE you the King that came to free us?"

Without hesitation Riel replied. "I am he. I have prayed this whole summer, hoping there was some way to change the Elegant. Their will is set against the Lord, and they don't even perceive it."

Lazarus almost fell from his tiny perch. This was the first time Riel had admitted to him that he was a King, and he was there to free them. He could hardly contain his joy, so he laughed out loud. Riel quickly laughed too and added an effective cough so the spies would not know he was speaking to Lazarus.

Riel said, "I must get to the far side of the valley to talk with Lawrence, Uriel, and Fammy, and I must bring Mini with me. I will need time alone with them to make sure our plans are clear. I am followed and always observed Lazarus."

"Who are you speaking about?" asked Lazarus.

"Two of them are a male and female Filk bears and then a black and white Donkey."

"The Prophecy is real? There really are Filk bears and a striped donkey like in the painting?"

"Exactly. The painting you showed me is exact."

"It's all true? All of it? But why did you wait all summer to reveal this to me? Did you not know when you saw the painting?"

"I was told by the Lord himself to be extremely careful and pray on each decision I would make," said Riel. "I had to observe too and see if the Elegant would repent of their ways. Everyone needs at least a chance to change. I have spent hours talking with King Kester about mercy and forgiveness, but when I come to the Sloven his whole demeanor changes, and he dismisses me. Their whole society is based on accumulation, competition, lies and intrigue. How many times has he complimented me on your beating?"

"I think the King has mentioned taking you on a hunt again?" Lazarus settled back into his perch.

"Yes. I have avoided them so far," said Riel. "I hate killing anything. I have had to fake beat Joshua several times too and that bothers me because it is also deceptive. Am I as deceptive as they are?"

"It is the only thing keeping them from realizing you are the King foretold in the Prophecy," said Lazarus. "If they knew who you were, they would murder you. Astar and the King have you in mind for marriage. They know you are more than you appear. Their greedy nature has blinded them to the Prophecy coming true before their very eyes."

Mini crawled out of Riel's pocket and without being visible to the wall behind them, made her way down the railing, into the vine and plopped herself squarely in Lazarus' lap. She gazed into Lazarus' smiling face and said, "You know they will be hunting wild if they see a Filk bear here in this valley? It has been 200 years since one came down from the mountains and the King will want his trophy."

"Ah, I see your meaning Mini! But first we must devise a way to free Riel enough to get him to the animals," replied Lazarus.

"It has been a difficult summer for all of us but now we need to plan and set things in motion." Riel stroked his chin in thought.

"Riel, I have caught a ride out to the edge of the Valley. Even now Uriel, Fammy and Lawrence are waiting on you. We have devised a plan together. But you need to speak to all of us, so we are very clear. They will kill us all if they even get a whiff of our actions." Mini got out of the vine and went back up into Riel's pocket.

Lazarus said, "Good grief does your marmot have plans before we even are ready to move?"

"She always thinks ahead and saved my life against the Black Dragon, Lazarus. I'd listen to her before anyone else," replied Riel.

"I will alert Uriel, Fammy and Lawrence," said Mini. "Filk droppings will be found at the northern end of the Valley furthest from the Citadel the day after tomorrow. That should cause a major stir and bring a host of the Elegant riding at full pelt. I bet they even include most of the guards that man the top of the castle. No one would want to miss that." Mini had a shrewd look on her tiny face.

"Then what?" Both Lazarus and Riel spoke in unison.

"You peel off from them when they are distracted and meet us at the South end. We can have Sloven set up to watch too. We will set our plans then, but I saw the Sloven below and they are an ingenious and intelligent group. You know I was down in the pit for half the summer. We worked together and many things have been set in order. And now, I think I know a way to free them."

Two days later, a horn was sounded at the northern end of the valley. Kester stopped in his tracks, then ran down an adjacent tunnel to look out a window. He saw two riders coming a full speed on their horses, so he ran all the way down to the entry gates. He waited anxiously, hopping on one foot for five minutes for them to get up the causeway and report.

"KIng Kester, we have found leavings of a huge animal. The oldest tracker we have says It appears to be a Filk bear." The soldier bowed as he said this.

Kester leapt straight up in the air. The people around him were so surprised as he was known to be stoic never excitable, nor demonstrative. "So, I am the keeper of the Prophecy! I knew it when they predicted the comet would appear the end of this month. I knew I was destined for greatness! So now my reign will dominate our history. I knew it was ME! I will conquer the great Filk. Now the savior of the Sloven will not come for a thousand years and I will rule over all! Bow before me Elegant!

"BOW! I and my daughter will rule in majesty and your great, great grandchildren will speak our names with reverence. Prepare the horses we have bred for this and alert the Guard."

The General had come down the next morning to watch the preparations. Beautiful black stallions were stamping in excitement, men were running helter-skelter with supplies, weapons and wagons were being loaded. The King always demanded fresh hot food, so a cook was always included. Tents, arms, cooking implements and anything else that might be necessary was being loaded and prepared.

The General approached Kester. "You are most worthy of the title Emperor Kester." He bowed deeply and continued, "It is approaching nightfall and we cannot track the bear at night. They are far too stealthy. Would you not prefer to sleep in your own bed this night?"

"I have given my commands now follow them." Kester was a picture of impatience sitting on his mobile throne in the gateway. He kept switching positions and tapping his feet.

"What of Riel, my liege? He prepares to ride with us. We still do not know of his alliances, and he wanders our halls, eats our food, courts our woman as if he is one of us."

"That is exactly why I am the King, and you are only my General. Do you not know that when he accompanies us on this hunt, he will return to his own land and spread the word about the Elegant. He will take Astar as his wife, and we will form an alliance to dominate the world. My glorious name will resound thought the Earth. Small minds like yours will be left without a history. Bring me my stallion, Windrider. Also bring Windring for Riel. He must keep up with me so he can record all these events."

The General stood for a moment in disbelief. Windring was one of the finest horses ever to be bred by the Elegant besides Windrider, the King's horse. Both horses had barrel chests and huge rippling muscles and could outrun any horse in the whole Kingdom. Why would the King give a visitor this horse to ride? He did not like it at all but there was nothing he could do but comply.

Riel came out the gate. They presented him with the animal to Riel's surprise. He had never seen a horse of such grandeur and beauty. He approached the huge animal with caution making crooning sounds in a sing song cadence, singing, "My beauty, my midnight sky, light of my life."

The horse eyed him. Riel handed him some grain, eventually rubbed his muzzle, and then laid his forehead against the beast. Windring whispered, "Oh stop Riel. I am your horse and have been since birth. The star on my forehead is a symbol to match the coming comet. Mini has told me of your exploits so far and now you have a worthy steed. What was all that sing-song stuff?"

Riel smiled and again laid his head against the horse's forehead whispering, "You are still the finest animal I ever had the privilege to ride, Windring."

"Yes, I am your finest horse, Riel. And I think we will have merry day taking these gentlemen on a ride. Mini has talked to all of us but you need to make sure all our plans are clear and well thought out." The horse snickered and said, "Look at King Kester, strutting around in his regal outfit with all those feathers, giving everyone directions. He's like a looney peacock."

Riel couldn't help but smile again. Soon they were off, but it was too late in the day, and they only managed to get to the Windrift River because the camp took hours to set-up. The King was very disappointed and yelled at anyone within earshot, so everyone avoided his tent. The next morning before the sun even thought about coming over the horizon, the King was dancing in impatience as his tent was collapsed and the others grabbed something to eat. Kester was the first one to be served as always.

They were off just as morning broke. It was going to be a fine end-of-summer day, a little cool with a fine breeze. Everyone's mood improved now they were moving. They were led to the bear scat and the King surveyed the low hills in front of him and the distant mountains. "Send five of our finest trackers and see where our friend is going" he commanded from his horses back. That set the pace for the remainder of the day as the trail led deep into the hills and farther and farther from the Citadel. That evening, the King held counsel.

The King relaxed by the fire, sitting on a stool looked at his General and said, "We know the animal is traveling towards the mountains, but do you think we can catch him?"

The General knew the scat was at least three days old but hesitated to tell the truth as he did not relish the thought of being posted in the stocks. So, he said, "Yes, there is no one more competent than you to do this feat."

Riel knew Uriel, Fammy and Lawrence were at the other end of the Valley waiting for him, but the Elegant were going in the opposite direction. Tonight, he planned to go to them as the guard had become relaxed and he had already found him sleeping during the last night watch. When everyone bedded down, Riel watched until he saw his guard breathing deeply, his head forward on his chest. He was near the edge of camp but still there were sentries. He carefully wound his way through the sleeping men and out to Windring.

"Took you long enough Riel," the horse quietly said when he approached. "There is one guard that we need to avoid. He is most serious about his job and is very alert. We will have to go around to the other side of the camp and then make our way out."

Riel untied Windring but he led him until they were well clear. It was not easy traveling in the dark but soon the moon rose, and the way was somewhat illuminated. The horse knew the way back and easily made it back to first camp and beyond by sunrise. They skirted the Valley and met the animals later that afternoon.

Mini's plan unfolded as the tasks to be completed were listed and organized. Lazarus had managed to get to the meeting also, as his people's part was integral to their freedom. Riel made sure all of them knew where to be and their place in the coming days.

Riel returned to the Citadel. The next day the whole troop returned with the King whose sour countenance could shrivel a lemon.

He was extremely perturbed with Riel and had him brought to him with handcuffs accompanied by several guards.

"You deceiver leaving our camp in the night! Why would you do such a thing after we have treated you as our guest," inquired the red-faced King. "I should just have your head lopped off and your body thrown down the cliff."

Riel looked perplexed. "Why have you handcuffed me? I thought I was your guest not a prisoner! I don't sleep well in the company of many others and simply wanted to return to my quiet room and bed after two days following you through bushes. I didn't know you needed a report on my whereabouts! I came back to the Citadel so it obvious I considered myself a guest." Riel feigned hurt and surprise.

The King softened a little. "You knew you were to report if you wanted to leave. We were hot on the trail, and I thought you'd be as excited as I was. It is my karma to fulfill my destiny here." He saw Astar peeking around a pillar, and she was shooting him "Daddy" looks.

"OH, I heard your men saying the skat was old and we were on a wild goose chase," Riel said. "I was getting very tired and almost fell off my horse, and the noise in camp was keeping me awake so I choose to not disturb any of you and go back to the Citadel."

"I'd like to know how you got past the sentries."

"I just tried to be quiet and not disturb any of you. Especially you Kester, I knew you needed your rest." Riel looked very innocent and saddened by the situation. The King felt uneasy, but he decided he needed a night in his bed as he was tired of camping too. He had them release Riel and he went to his chambers.

The General whispered in Riel's ear as he unlocked the cuffs, "You are up to something you sneaky bastard, I can feel it. My eyes are on you from here on out."

Riel turned and smiled in his face and said, "What can one man do against the full force of the Elegant and their army?"

Three days later, again the trumpets were sounded to the north and the riders came swiftly to the King. This time, there was an actual glimpse of the beast, and the preparations were much swifter. They managed to get the whole entourage out of the Castle in a few hours. The sighting was near the same place.

This time Riel seemingly took very ill indeed, and the King's doctor went to see him, just before the trumpets sounded.

Riel had taken a concoction Lazarus provided and he had thrown up all morning. When the Doctor walked in Riel managed to heave particularly in his direction. The Doctor reported that Riel would not be going anywhere for the next few days.

Down in the stables, Windring was assigned to a rider of high standing in the courts. The horse was having none of it: He bucked and danced until the Nobel told the stable master to leave him be and he selected a gentler animal. The General had observed Riel and the horse during their first outing and was standing there noting the horse's demeanor now. He thought back and remember the horse almost seemed to be talking to Riel and that he mounted the beast with ease. He put his forehead on the horse and the horse didn't react. This whole thing was going wrong somehow. The Prophecy has many interpretations according to one's history, background, and circumstances. The real message of the Prophecy is that justice will one day prevail, and, in the end, love is the answer. It may not be in our time frame or to our flavor, but God's will eventually win out.

The Elegant were committing most of their resources to the hunt and the forces left behind would not be able to control the Sloven if they got out of hand. The King as undisputed ruler wanted everyone along but how could the General make sure his home was safe? He headed for the guardhouse.

The King had Etriel's harness brought out from the vaults along with his ermine overcoat, chains of gold for his neck, a pure gold scepter and his gem encrusted crown. Etriel's harness was made of finely wrought filigree and encrusted with rose-cut diamonds that sparkled even in a dark room. The servants had to scrub off the dust from these long unused items. The harness was over 300 years old and said to bring luck and good fortune.

The King relished wearing them and took great pride in dressing and preparing.

The General ordered everyone except a small contingent force to go but he purposely stayed behind and doubled the spies looking in on Riel. The men who drew this duty were very unhappy with the General. The captain in particular, was perturbed.

Sparkling like the sun King Kester led the hundreds of Elegant down the causeway and off down the road towards the mountains. The guards left behind on top of the Cliff were waving at the procession below. Family crests unfurled in the wind, blowing horns and trumpets accented an atmosphere of pure fanfare.

The whole contingent was surrounded by their wives, children and friends who were throwing flowers at the men on horses

Unknown to the Elegant, deep below and at the back of the Citadel a hive of activity was taking place: wagons loaded with supplies waited behind thin rock walls ready to be demolished. The Sloven were waiting for the signal with huge sledgehammers to open the way to freedom.

Already the ladders were hoisted into the open ceiling in the Mathematic's laboratory. Horses neighed and whinnied in the confined spaces as they were being harnessed and loaded.

Elderly Sloven were loaded into several comfortable pillowed carts which included umbrellas and a snack basket. The children were waiting too but they were in much larger wagons along with a few supplies. All of them waited on Riel for the signal.

Riel took the antidote and drank a large glass of water. Lazarus was in the vine waiting for him. Riel was still very queasy when he walked over to the terrace. He could see a distant puff of dust from the Elegant. They were still too close, and he was still not feeling too good. He said, "I can see the distant stragglers Lazarus. We better wait a little more. Did you put the drugs in the water supply?"

"Hours ago, Riel," said Lazarus. "I made sure yours was not contaminated though. You'll feel much better in about twenty minutes. But you will need more water, so go get another glass of water from the jug." Riel complied and returned.

"Is almost everyone asleep by now?" Riel asked.

"Yes, already most of the Elegant are safely snoring on their couches and beds," said Lazarus.

"They will wake tomorrow not feeling too good, but they will all be alive. We could have poisoned and killed them all but thank God, we have hearts and celebrate the Lord. That is not who we are as a people."

Riel felt a wave of pride towards the Sloven. Riel surveyed the mirror wall and found two sets of eyes watching his every move. He burped loudly and held his stomach retreating to the bath area.

An hour later, the General was walking through the city and noticed it was far too quiet, even for having so many on the hunt. No children out playing and why were the stoops vacant on a day to celebrate? He decided to check a few houses, but no one answered his knock. He ran directly to the cliff towers to check on the archers and guards. There was no movement when he arrived through the open gate. A breech to begin with. He ran to the first tower and found the men there sleeping hunched over against the walls.

He shook the first man he came to, but the man just slumped over on the ground. He happened to look over the wall and nearly fell over: Below, beyond belief were hundreds of Sloven forming what could only called a wagon train. Holes in the walls of the pit showed even more activity.

Where did that many of the little pigs come from? The lead wagon was already heading away in the opposite direction of the Elegant. He turned to find ten Sloven facing him with nasty smiles on their faces. Lazarus was one of them, but he looked healthy and full of vigor. What was going on?

"We want you to see something special General," Lazarus spit out the words. They bound him and half dragged him to the Lyon's Gates below.

There at the gate sat Astar gagged and tied to the arms of her moveable throne. Her hair was tied into several tightly bound knots on top of her head. She had pointed huge dark circles around her eyes and her mouth was colored bright red three times larger than her actual lips. The Sloven had put their clothes on her which were covered with dirt, way too small even for her tiny frame. A Sloven woman was removing her gold earrings as Astar looked defiant and tried to twist away. The woman said, "Had it not been for Riel and his orders, I personally would have thrown you from your own balcony. I saw you throw my daughter off that horrible day you 'culled our herd.' Today, it was him that ordered that YOU were not to be harmed. I don't know why; you are worse than any viper and God help you for the children you have killed and thrown away."

The General turned around and could not believe his eyes. There standing in front of the Gate was a Filk bear accompanied by the biggest donkey he had ever seen with black and white stripes all over his body. Fammy looked the evil man right in his eyes and lumbered up to him. She got extremely close to his face and then sniffed his hair. His hair almost stood on end but was too confined and long. He felt his bowels release as her hot breath fanned over his closed eyes. A combination of Fammy's breath and her incredible size and smell overwhelmed his unbelieving eyes.

"Oh dear, the poor lad has had an accident. I thought my movements were sweet, but his take on an added flavor," exclaimed Lawrence sniffing the air in disgust.

The General could not believe that now, he was hearing animals talking. "Where did you two come from? How can I understand you?"

"I don't believe we owe you any explanation considering your current position. However, I will tell you that Riel will always be our Master and you might consider the paintings in the caverns below. Now just let me check that you are tightly bound." With that, Fammy took her mammoth razor-sharp claws, waved them right in front of the General's face, and checked the ropes were locked tight.

The General just kept from fainting but his eyesight was swimming with closing black walls but as Fammy checked the tension he just fainted dead away.

Lazarus looked at the General's limp body. Smirking Lawrence said, "The poor boy is limp and wet too."

Lazarus said, "If Riel had heard that line he would not be pleased. You are so silly for Donkey, and what an attitude. We've got children below and all of us must be out of here in a few hours. Can you go reconnoiter and report back?" Lawrence held his tail high in the air galloping a little sideways out the main gate.

"What shall we do with the General," inquired the Sloven woman.

"Set him right beside Astar and bind their chairs together. She should really enjoy that smell. In fact, they have had relations for many years anyways and they may as well be bound in this way too." Lazarus took a savory moment to consider before he walked off to help below.

"And you told the Donkey to be quiet?" The woman signaled to two nearby Sloven and they man-handled the general into position to the disgust and reversion of Astar.

Some miles distant, the entourage was having a gay time anticipating the killing of the bear. Conversation was limited because it was almost dark, and they had to ride more cautiously. Kester tended to ride out in front at some speed and then must slow down because he could not see much.

The result was a line of horses who had to stop and start with gaps in between. At midnight, the King finally gave up with the slow progress and ordered everyone to stop.

The Sloven provided a hasty meal of vegetable soup, tiny cakes, and fresh fruit. King Kester was pacing back and forth in front of his tent.

"Have you ever seen such a slow procession as this one? I think I will ride ahead with a small contingent in the morning. Let the rest hunt for themselves!" The four guards next to him were nodding in agreement.

The Lieutenant said, "The Sloven are holding us up. They can hardly ride like we do, and it takes them forever to break and set-up camp. Look at tonight! That meal was hardly gourmet, and they are just now getting everyone to bed. We should pack our saddlebags with food and head out fast in the morning."

Kester thought about all the inconvenience, but it did please him to leave everyone in the dust. He wondered if he could sleep on a bedroll, but he was game to find out. And frankly, he was tired of the Sloven hanging around him.

He wanted that bear, and he was going to get him. The King called the leader of the Sloven to his tent. He hit the little man several times before saying, "You and your mongrel dogs and savages have held up our whole group with your slowness. You leave a few of you to attend the others and the rest of you pathetic useless things return to the Citadel after breakfast. I will have an appropriate punishment ordered when I return with the bear."

He hit the Sloven again.

The Sloven said, "Oh my King, can we not watch you slay the mighty Filk?" He had a fresh bleeding welt across his tiny face.

"Get ALL your filthy little slobs together and get out before I have this guard shoot an arrow through your useless heart. Get OUT! All of you…"

The King was now in a rage and very tired.

The Sloven bedded the troops down but then in a swift action left the camp before the King's order could be reversed. The next morning was utter chaos. No one knew how to get the food cooked on the fire, the horses were unmanageable, they were unable to fold the tents or store them, essentially, assembling the Elegant turned into a nightmare. The King was utterly disgusted and very impatient. He had twenty of his men get everything they needed, pack the saddlebags and bed rolls and leave. They chewed on mibre cakes as they rode.

Some of the Elegant threw caution to the wind and got up on their horses and rode like the wind but soon discovered lunch was not forthcoming and in their haste, they did not account for the supply problem. Some turned back to the camp.

A contingent of twenty was much easier riding and they began to really make some speed. The bear was only a day away and the scouts reported they had found his trail leading north.

The Citadel was wrapped in silence when the small group of Sloven returned to their once home. It took only a few minutes for them to collect the packs left for them at the Lyon's Gate. They were carefully watering their horses with fresh unpoisoned water and then planned to press on to the main Sloven group. However, while checking the city, the man who was whipped by the King for being slow and a couple of his men, spotted Astar tied up to the General in the Great Hall.

"Look at those two, ha, ha, ha. Look at Astar, now that is some makeup! Someone has done a great job."

Astar replied with hate in her eyes, "It is because of you little pigs that we are left here to die in our own filth. You are no better than your name implies."

The Sloven said, "You and the others press on ahead and get the stragglers moving. We will feed the General and Astar, let them wash and retie them and catch up to you. We have the fastest horses anyway and you may as well encourage more speed as it does not look like they left that long ago."

They untied the two Elegants, allowed them a quick cleaning, gave them both water and allowed them a piece of fruit and a small cake, and then tied the two back in their chairs. The water was lightly drugged with the last of the potion and soon both were asleep again, the General snoring rather loudly.

The last Sloven closed the Lyon's Gate and repelled down from the guard's window high above to the causeway.

Anything to delay the Elegant might make a difference. Then the last three took off in a flurry to circle to the back of the Cliff Castle and retrieve their waiting mounts. A line of pots, pans, household items were strewn haphazardly all over the road. They had to pick their way forward but soon the way was clearer, and they picked up speed. An hour later they caught up with the others they had sent ahead. An hour later they saw Lazarus who was waiting for them.

"How goes it?" Lazarus yelled into the wind as his men approached him. "The Elegant are all sleeping or on the hunt and much delayed. But what happened, you should be much further south than this."

"We had a hard time getting some of the wagons out of the main cave.

"The openings were harder to collapse than we thought. The hidden ones cannot bear the sunlight and so we had to devise bags and covers for their eyes. However, we are all moving now, and the line is over twenty miles ahead of us. I need you to encourage these stragglers and get them moving. I have an idea to slow the hunting party too. Can you two follow me and help?" He pointed to two of the Sloven that were helping him earlier in the day.

"I told you sending the Sloven away and taking off in a small group was a good idea," said the Lieutenant to the King. He was right behind the Monarch as they stopped for a brief rest.

The King turned on his horse, the man was behind him so he looked as far as he could. "That was my idea," stormed the King. King Kester was very hungry by this time, and he had really missed his break for afternoon tea cakes and cut sandwiches. The thought of stale Mibre or journey cakes made him sick to his stomach. A distant horn sounded. His stomach was forgotten, as a well of excitement passed through the twenty.

"They have found the trail of the bear," the King shouted in glee.

All of them starting shouting and spurring their horses. They met the scouts at the next hill's crown.

The scout was practically dancing in his saddle when he said, "We have found fresher droppings my King!" There between them was a huge pile of bear feces.

"That must be some bear to have that big of a diamond pile!" Word passed down the Valley eliciting hoots and whistling and efforts to catch up to the King's lead.

The King shouted, "The chase begins!" The group of twenty, who had been milling around the skat, took off north passing the King himself in their frenzy.

Trumpets were blaring, men were shouting and the echoes off the surrounding hills sounded like an army approached. Uriel would have to be deaf, dumb, and stupid not to hear what was chasing him.

The scouts found a second fresher pile that very evening. Kester forgot about eating and spurred his horse to a gallop passing his own scouts in the process. The group that managed to get to camp that night were tired to the bone, hungry and not happy about trying to set up camp after dark. Kester was far too worked up to sleep and sought out his Lieutenant.

"I am restless. Tomorrow my destiny maybe fulfilled," he said.

"You are fearless, my liege. A King for the Ages! The man that history will remember." The Lieutenant was a man of exaggeration.

"Did you leave the men we talked about behind at the Castle?" Kester asked.

"Yes, it was a small group insisted on by your paranoid General, I made the men that drew my ire in the past stay behind with him. I cannot imagine how upset they were to be left behind on this historic quest," said the Lieutenant. He snickered.

The King snickered too. "How soon do you think we will see this phenomenal bear? Have we any reports tonight?"

"They hope to catch a sighting tomorrow. He is nearby and his diamonds are sparkling fresh. I am told the beast is truly a monster. They have seen his prints in the Windrift River mud. We must navigate to a safer crossing tomorrow," said the Lieutenant.

"Is the water too swift even on these horses? We must not lose valuable time," said Kester. "Let us be on with it. AND, you better tell your men it is my arrow that will foster the animal's death and no other. If anyone raises a finger to it, they will be hanged when we return to the Citadel."

"As you command," said the Lieutenant. "But some have already gone ahead tonight. Remember we cannot replace you and you are more valuable than any animal."

The King was trying to decide if that was a compliment. "Round every one of them up yourself tonight and no one but the scouts are to be in front of me ever again."

"But I am hungry and tired. Can we not do this in the morning? You are always so thoughtful and kind to us, cannot you wait those few hours?" asked the Lieutenant.

"Well, I guess we are all tired. Yes, send for them in the morning but first thing," said Kester.

"And don't think I will let you off the hook again either." A huge lengthy yawn escaped the King, and he looked to see who was getting his bedroll ready.

The King was not long snoring in his bedroll when two of his entourage took pleasure in blaring their horns right beside his sleeping form. The King, dreaming of his concubine, was so startled he jumped straight up and began running towards the horses. His bedclothes were left behind and he looked around in fear thinking the bear had invaded the camp. "What the hell," he shouted.

A scout approached him. "You will never believe this my liege." The Lieutenant bowed but it was too dark to see.

The King, now shaking from the cold breeze going up his skivvies, replied, "What idiot blew his horn in my ear and what the hell is going on!"

"Apparently Riel has tracked us after he recovered and has gone on ahead after the bear," said the Lieutenant. "We found fresh horse tracks from Windring, Bear tracks and evidence of a violent encounter."

"I don't believe it! I just don't believe it! How could he get in front of us? Encounter? You said encounter? What the God's green earth is going on here?" The King grabbed a man's blanket from the ground and wrapped himself in it. The man shocked by the cold air, started stamping the ground and looking for his clothing.

"As near as we can make out tonight, Riel has tracked the bear in front of us before the scouts even knew he was here," said the Lieutenant. "He is in front of us and there was evidence of a scuffle in which the bear was injured. Both are across the Windrift River already. We think Riel is even now near capturing the animal."

The King finally recovering from the cold and the rude awakening, finally started thinking rationally. "Awake the camp, bring me my horse, get us something to eat quickly and we shall leave as soon as we can. I will determine what to do to our friend when we find him and the bear." The King had an evil gleam in his eyes when he set out at the breaking dawn.

The cavalcade got to the Windrift River a few hours later where the current was swift and deep. Across the water, two scouts were pointing up from where they were standing on the shore. A steep cliff covered in brush and vegetation rose 500 feet above the water. Up on the top dirt and dust was in the air and a terrific fight was going on. At least that was the appearance of it. Screams were heard then silence.

Suddenly the dust cleared and Riel's form in a defensive position, sword drawn, was backing towards the cliff edge. The angry bear, standing up on his hind legs, fully 12-feet tall, teeth barred was almost upon the man. Then more screams. The bear's chest had three arrows sticking out of his breastbone and he was bleeding profusely. His mouth was full of froth, and he was growling so loud even the King heard it. It was only a few seconds later as the bear picked Riel up and tossed him ten feet in the air off the left side of the cliff. Riel cleared a nearby tree in the process. His sword clanged useless to the ground.

"Well, I guess that is the end of our alliance hopes. He deserved that end: Imagine racing ahead of me, the King! We need to cross the Windrift River and kill that beast before he kills anyone else." One of the scouts pointed upstream and they soon assembled looking for a safe passage.

The King, now frightened of the huge beast, ordered three of his skilled archers to accompany him at the front. They soon found a way and managed to drift most of the way back to the cliff face where they came back onto the further shore. Here his scouts met him.

"My liege, we have not found a way to get up the face of this cliff with our horses. The bear is obviously hurt and losing blood. The only way up is to take the path along the shore and backtrack to a safer path."

Just then another scout appeared on his horse. "We found the way up my Lord." They all raced along the shore and managed to wind up the cliff from the backside. The scene above was horrific: A large area was effectively demolished. The brushes were broken off, the ground strewn with rocks, the plants destroyed, even a small tree was broken at the trunk but most telling, a trail of dripping blood led off north. Dark bloodstained ground was everywhere. The Scouts looked down the cliff where Riel was thrown but could not see a body below for the vegetation and trees.

Earlier, while the King and his subjects were finding a way to cross the Windrift River, Riel said, "The game is afoot, Uriel. Now we have got to hurry. It won't take the Scouts long to find the path up the backside."

Mini ran into camp. "I've dripped blood for as long as I could north, but you two will have to break off branches and leave some paw prints to convince these scouts."

Riel was unwinding the wire around the bear that held the three arrows in Uriel's chest. He also took off the furry bag of blood underneath the bear's arm.

Then, Riel and Uriel worked feverishly on the ledge where Riel landed where they had put pine boughs to break his fall. They both carefully shimmied over the lip and working feverishly threw the branches further down slope, so they were not visible.

They then took the furry bag of blood and finished it off by dripping it on the ledge and added some over the edge. Then, they worked their way off the mesa traveling north leaving Uriel prints here and there and several blood drips. They made sure all other prints were wiped away with a cut off bush. They went to the trail's end and beyond where the mountains started their upward climb. Finally, they were done, Riel mounted Windring, Mini got between Uriel's ears and they were off a full speed for the Citadel, skirting the edges where they knew the Elegant were headed.

One Scout was let down to the ledge Riel should have landed on. He was very confused: Riel's body was nowhere to be found even looking over the edge. The blood proved the man could not have survived the toss or the fall. But something was not right about the whole scene. The Scout had tracked animals all his life and something just didn't feel right about the scene above or the ledge or even the absence of Riel's body. He hollered up to the King, who was standing ten feet above him: "There is lots of blood above and even here.

"We all saw the bear throw Riel over that tree and down off this cliff. But I don't see any evidence of him landing but a patch of dried blood in the dirt. I'm not sure what is going on."

"Forget Riel, get back up here and let's get that bear. He could not have got far with three arrows sticking in his chest," replied the King.

The lieutenant standing behind the King said, "I don't know, your grace."

"That bear looked mighty mad, and the arrows didn't seem to be a bother tossing Riel around like he was a rag doll. That bear looks like he will chew us up and spit us out. I'd go forward with caution if I were you."

"Well, where are my archers?" the King asked. "They should be able to do some serious damage from a distance. Are they in that single file path leading up the damned cliff face?

"How are we supposed to get going with all this chaos happening?" The King stomped over to his horse and mounted. "I will finish off what Riel started, and I will do it today!"

Two more scouts arrived and surveyed the scene and the ledge from above, both looked perplexed. They formed a circle and softly whispered among themselves. The lead walked up to the King and looking concerned said, "Oh my Mighty Ruler, would that you listen for a moment. All three of us agree that something about this cliff and ledge is not ringing right. We urge you to use great caution in moving forward."

"What is the ringing you don't think is right?" exclaimed the King. "I am not sitting here discussing blood on the ground when we should be moving in all haste to kill this dangerous and deadly beast." The King was so irritated he kicked his horse to get something moving. The animal shot off circling the mesa, while the scouts scrambled to follow the blood trail. The lead man assigned one scout to remain behind and study the cliff and ledge area in detail sending word forward when he reached his conclusions. The King, hyperventilating at this point, ordered everyone off the single file trail so he could go down and get the whole menagerie in gear.

It took them two hours to come to the end of the blood trail where it just simply stopped. The Scouts were remarking that for that size injured bear, the trail was remarkably clean of damage and the paw prints seemed haphazard like they were staged. Now the blood just stopped and there was no sign of the bear and where was Windring?

The Lead Scout approached the King. He bowed but his face was white with consternation, "King Kester, something is very wrong about this whole thing. There is no real damage on this trail from the bear, not many imprints on the ground, nothing but a clear blood trail almost evenly spaced from here back to the cliff. There is no sign of the animal here at all where the blood just simply stops."

Kester stopped and started scratching his head. HIs heart started to race. His suspicions taking over his mind, he said, "Let us return to the Cliff and see what really occurred there. You are right. Something is very, very wrong about this whole thing. How does a blood trail just stop in the middle of nowhere when the animal had three arrows in his chest?"

They all returned post haste. The scout that remained looked downcast and defeated when they returned. "The word is not good, our worthy Elegant Leader. Look at this wire with the arrows attached." He handed the King the arrows. "The wire is just long enough to go around the bear's girth and the arrows were tied without heads. We found a furry bag which had the blood in it, halfway down the cliff in the foliage. We also found several chopped pine branches. The thing that was wrong that all of us Scouts sensed was that there is far too much blood on this battlefield. Enough for five men and two bears. We just didn't realize until now what was truly going on. We have all been deceived!"

The King shaking his head in disgust said, "The whole thing was staged, but why?"

"Yes Sir, it was staged and for some cause," said the Lead Scout.

Then the King remembered the painting in the Sloven cavern. He realized it was Riel standing with the bear in that painting. Then he remembered the boots Riel was wearing the first day he saw the man. The beaded designs on them were so unique and different.

They were partially concealed by the painting stick figures applied over them, but now he realized he never saw those boots on Riel ever again. How could he, the King, be so stupid? Riel had not warmed to Astar, he roamed the Castle at leisure, he spied on their meetings, he ate their food but what was the man's goal? Then the whole truth of the situation dawned on him.

Riel was freeing the Sloven and because of the General's request he had left only a small contingent force to control the little pigs. He would punish the man when he returned for not thinking more clearly about safety.

"Mount your steeds," shouted the King. "We return to the Citadel as quickly as possible. We have been had by those sick, twisted little bastards, the Sloven. Riel is a traitor and worthy of crucifixion when we catch the rotten liar. You had better ride like you never have before because if the Sloven are freed, all of us are going to suffer."

They tried to ride, but between their tired horses and incompetence it was nothing like Riel, Uriel and Mini had achieved. The King's group had to stop that evening as they were all starving, their horses winded and hungry and everyone was complaining and nasty to each other. It was far from a pleasant atmosphere and all of them had to sleep on the ground, which further enraged them all.

The next morning the lieutenant gingerly approach the King. "My most worthy King, oh ruler of the mighty Elegant, I need to approach and discuss a problem."

"Do we not have enough problems?" said Kester. "What is it?"

"Sir, we are concerned for our safety but more concerned about yours. There are only twenty of us here and we must wait until we have sufficient forces to approach the Citadel. We have no clue what has happened there and what forces we face. Our wives and children may all be dead by now."

The King had not thought about this and in his anger realized he maybe jeopardizing his life. He thought about Astar in the hands of those animals and his rage mounted even more. What could he do? There was a string of men behind him. He would have to wait until he had enough of them to defend himself.

They waited until noon in the camp when several others caught up with them. It felt good to get a decent hot meal, which the Lieutenant put together. The king had his horse fed and rested and some of the others stayed in their bedrolls until they had to ride again.

In the meantime, Riel arrived at the Citadel that noon. He stopped at the Lyon's gate but found the entrance closed and locked. It was dead silent, and nothing moved anywhere. It gave Riel a chill. He was preparing to go around to the back when he noted the General's face in the guard window above the gate.

He started to turn Windring around when an arrow shot through the air. Suddenly, Mini leaped from the saddle horn and covered Riel's chest with her body. She was pinned to Riel's chest with an arrow, the blood gurgling out of her mouth and with her tiny face turned up to Riel she said, "Ride on Riel and save the Sloven. I give my life freely." She went limp, her face falling forward and then her body fell into Riel's lap. He road to the wall out of range and removed the arrow from her chest, held her close for a moment of grief, dismounted Windring and then placed her body in his saddle bag.

Rage covered Riel's face as he mounted Windring. Uriel stood in the way. "We must get the Sloven to safety, Riel, not avenge Mini's sacrifice. We don't know what has happened and how far they have gone."

"You go ahead and check the Sloven. I will get the man that took Mini's life." Uriel looked at Riel's face and moved aside. Riel rode to the vine and climbed two hundred feet straight up and exited onto a terrace inside the Castle. The couple living there had just woke up from drugged stupor and saw him cross to their front door. They were left behind in even more confusion. All over the Citadel, Elegant were beginning to wake. They had no clue what happened, but they were loopy and had terrible headaches. Most of them went back to bed but a few noticed many of their valuables gone and not a Sloven available to serve them.

Uriel knew he had to get going and Windring was prancing in place at the wall. "I have to go Windring, I can't think of anything I can do to help Riel."

"We can go to the back and see what happened. Perhaps they have left someone to report to us. Also, I need water and food Uriel. I am not a bear," said Windring.

Around the back they found the strewn supplies and trail of materials from the Sloven exodus. They found good water and food and took a few minutes to refresh themselves. Uriel jumped in the water trough, which split and fell apart with him in it. "Ah that felt good even if I only had a refreshing moment!" Uriel shook himself and found another stash of food, which he quickly consumed.

In the meantime, Riel heard noises above him and wound up a set of stairs. Then he quickly navigated to the main City. He saw the General was closing the gates to the Palace behind him, then the locks clicked. Riel crossed the distance across the City at a dead run, climbed the rock face to the right of the gold doors, and using the water duct from the roof, managed to get near a window in the Palace. A six-foot chasm opened in front of him. He threw every bit of might he had into the jump, but it was only enough to leave him hanging from the windowsill. It was at least 100 feet to the floor below. Then he remembered Mini's face as she died saving him. He hauled his weight up, sat on the sill, and entered the Palace. Again, he could hear footsteps on the floor above him. He ran out through the room and took the stairs to the roof top.

"I see even the little animals put their life before yours," exclaimed the General.

"You have no idea who you have murdered this day," replied Reil. "It was by my command that you and your worthless Elegant were not all slaughtered today. And if anyone deserved it, it was Astar and you, you arrogant and worthless human."

The General laughed out loud and put his sword at ready. Riel raised his sword also.

Gloating, the General said, "I bet you had good training, but you can't begin to match my years of experience. I have practiced every day since my youth and have won many battles. I have butchered the Sloven and taken their children for swordplay just to watch them die. You just don't have this in you."

"I may look like I have little training, but I tell you I was trained by Gabriel himself."

"What Gabriel would train a boy like you?" The General laughed.

"Gabriel has never seen defeat and conquered every army the Lord commanded him to. It is not I who is in mortal danger, it is you." At this, Riel began a series of graceful moves with his sword. The rapier was not ornate but was delicately balanced for Riel's hand alone.

The Captain watched, surprised as the sword air danced in front of him. The boy was good but had nothing on him.

"When did you meet this Gabriel and was it your intent to deceive him too?" the General asked.

"The Gabriel I am speaking of would know immediately if spoke anything untrue," said Riel. "I cannot deceive him as I have done with your foolish, insolent, wasteful, entitled, overbearing, mean-spirited and lazy people. I did not deceive for my own gain but for the Sloven who you have most brutally mistreated and enslaved. You are all lazy, stupid people who murdered and maimed innocent children and then went to Church to claim your superiority. You are not God's Chosen but a pack of lazy people, materialistic in all ways and sadist bastards." With berserker blood coursing through his veins, Riel attacked.

The General was just able to fend off Riel's attack. He started to feel an inkling of his opponent's prowess. They danced back and forth across the rooftop with the General using every known sword trick he could think of. Every ploy was anticipated and defended. Riel was limiting his attack to the skill of the General.

"Gabriel would call you a beginner!" Riel laughed as he deftly removed one of the general's buttons.

"A beginner I don't think so! Who is this, Gabriel?"

"You learn about him when you are studying the Bible, General. You talk about training from your youth, he's been in service for many centuries. The armies he faced were many times what you have here."

"The Captain of the Lord's Army?" the General asked.

"That is indeed who taught me," replied Riel with a terrible gleam in his eye.

He removed three more buttons from the General's service jacket. Then he cut off an epaulet, shredding the fringe in the process.

"You have lied to us all long and now I am to believe you were trained by the Lord's Commander?" said the General.

"If you stop and think about it, I have never lied to you even once General," said Riel. "You just assumed that I hated the Sloven. Here is the whip I beat Lazarus with." Riel took the little whip from his belt and threw it to the General across the space between them.

The General caught it in midair and felt the little soft pliable tips that looked like metal. "So even the whip was an utter lie."

"I never lied to you even once General," replied Riel in a cold, deep voice.

"Did you know I have bedded Astar many times?" said the General. "How many times have you had her?"

"I don't bed used goods General," said Riel. "And the son she conceived with you, hid from you was murdered a few hours after his birth. She did not want to be tied to you, a commoner."

"There was no son, another lie." Then the General realized Astar disappeared from court for a few months and returned as slender and beautiful as ever.

"She has had three children General. The first was your son. The other two after yours were sold into slavery for her convenience."

The General had heard rumors but, in his pillow talk and lovemaking with her, she claimed and acted as though she was a virgin hiding their liaison from her defensive and materialistic Father. The King had to be complicit in this too as he must have known about the children.

This angered the General and he lunged at Riel. Riel reacted so quickly he cut a gash in the General's arm and removed the other epaulette from his shoulder with the same sword sweep.

The next skirmish was intense, and the General came out of it winded. He started to realize he may not survive this battle. He'd never seen anyone handle a sword at Riel's level. If he could work Riel towards the Guard tower, perhaps one or two of them was awake enough to help him. Earlier he saw some of the residents staggering around looking very lost. If one of the soldiers could just distract the man.

"Where were you that you took these lessons from this Master Commander?" the General asked. "He is not a Master

Commander. Gabriel is the Prince of the host of Jehovah and I took those lessons in Paradise." Riel attacked and the General's sword clattered to the ground fifteen feet away. "Retrieve your weapon you fool," Riel said. "It took me long to learn that move, as it takes exceptional balance, and you must be able to move rapidly.

"This day you will pay for all the murdering, cheating, lying, and sinning you have committed in your life. You will find the arrow you used on Mini is nothing compared to how you will suffer now. Get your sword, you worthless piece of dung."

The General ran and picked up his sword but bolted to the Guard tower. Riel expected as much but knew all the military had been double dozed with potion and would not wake until tonight or tomorrow. Riel blocked the single door, so the General was trapped.

The General realizing said, "So my superior swordsman must you confine our battle to this small room where you have the advantage?"

Riel backed from the door and allowed the General to exit. However, the General kept right on running to the outside stairwell leading down into the Palace. Riel ran behind and caught up with him at a switchback. Riel removed the rest of the man's buttons in three quick trusts. "Remove your jacket, General. I wish to play a little more before I take your worthless life."

The General looked over the railing behind him into the Sloven pit and saw the Filk bear and Windring eating below. He took off his jacket and was glad for a moment because it cooled his body. He threw the jacket in Riel's face and ran back up the stairs.

Riel was upon him just as he reached the top. Riel began in earnest. The General, breathing heavy and realizing was not going to survive took twenty shallow cuts all over his body before the skirmish was complete. "Let me breathe, let me breathe!" he said.

Riel backed a few feet and allowed the man a moment. The Captain removed his undershirt to reveal a chest criss-crossed with numerous scars and burn marks. "Who has done that damage to you General?" Riel asked.

"You do not think I attained this rank by nothing other than sheer determination and the ability to take any pain my mentors inflicted?" the General said.

"You mean to tell me those scars are from your own people?" said Riel.

"My Father, but mostly the King who loved to cut me when I was a Captain, and every rank took another series of scars with it. I am proud of every one of them," said the General.

"But the burns? Why the burn marks?" asked Riel.

"See the biggest one here above my heart?" said the General. "That is done as my metal proclaiming to all that I am a General. It took a year to heal but my service was secured. I am the highest rank besides King Kester himself. Now, you have seen my badges and I have one final honor to offer."

Riel felt disgust for these people.

The General suddenly backed to the wall his sword held high. He let out a blood curdling scream and jumped over the wall falling hundreds of feet to his death. Riel looked over the railing to see his flattened bloody form far below. Uriel and Windring were staring up at him.

He knew others would soon be awake and he raced down the stairwell, through the corridors and across the throne room. Running through the further doors he ran right into Astar. She was thrown backwards against the wall and slumped to the floor.

He ran to her. Her hair was loose and framed her beautiful face, she looked up at a without one dot of make-up and said, "Do not leave me behind. I love you, Riel. You are the only man I have ever loved."

Riel looked into her fearful eyes and knew his heart was given to her. He tenderly touched her face and gave her a long, amorous kiss on her open lips. He also realized she was deceitful beyond belief. She returned his advance and put her soft persuasive lips on his and his whole being melted. He was disarmed by a woman. He kissed her back with such deep longing that had built over the summer, that she pressed against him, opening her passionate mouth to receive his tongue. He suddenly separated from her shaking his head, he realized he had smelled her potion, but it had been weakened by her fear and trauma over the last day. He looked into her love-soft eyes, took her tiny hands in his and said, "You cannot be trusted Astar. I have got to save the Sloven from your clutches and the hands of your merciless, sinful people, and your evil Father." He stood up releasing her.

"Not before I inflict harm on you," she shouted. A small dagger appeared in her hand, and she threw herself at Riel. He was quick but not quick enough and a small cut opened on his left arm before he could disarm her. She began to cry in earnest.

He left her in the hallway and ran all the way down to the Sloven pit.

Windring was there waiting for him, dancing with impatience. "Uriel left a few minutes ago," said Windring. "Look at all the debris the Sloven have left behind. I wonder if we have saved them or doomed them, Riel? It looks like they took much longer than we thought to empty the Citadel and you know the King is going to be right behind us. Why did the General jump? We watched him and we know you did not push him over."

"The man had no way out. He jumped to preserve his dignity before I could cut him down," said Riel.

"What took you so long?" Windring asked.

"I saw Astar on the way down and enjoyed the fight so much, I lost track of time," said Riel.

"Well fortunately, I am the best of the horses and I have had time to eat, rest and drink water. Did you at least drink something up there?"

"Everything had potion in it," said Riel.

"Well fortunately, Uriel thought of that and filled both your canteens from the fresh water flowing into the cistern. Might I suggest a draft before we engage the road?" said Windring.

Riel drank long and deep and jumped onto Windring. They took off slow because the obstructions on the road but soon picked up speed. "How fast can you make this without injuring yourself Windring?" Windring snorted and soon the Citadel was out of sight behind them.

That evening they came around a bend and there was Uriel standing in the middle of the road. "My God man, where have you been?"

"We got here as quickly as we could. Where is Lazarus?" said Riel.

"Up ahead waiting for you at the campfire. What happened at the Castle that you took so long? Did the General jump as we thought?"

Riel spurred Windring and they closed the distance quickly. Riel dismounted.

Lazarus and several the Sloven all ran to Riel and attached themselves to his body and his legs. "We are moving better now Riel. Most of us are more than twenty miles ahead but there are many stragglers. We thought something happened to you. We all heard about Mini. Your sorrow is our sorrow. We know how much she meant to you," remarked Lazarus, sorrow coloring his face.

Riel had felt the sting of loss. She no longer sat on his saddle horn asking him questions, commenting on life, devising her plans. Riel felt sad and a tear escaped onto his cheek. He felt very tired suddenly, but he wanted to pray. It had been a grueling few days, and he must take tonight to rest and recover.

He circled the camp walking and praying and then sat down on a small stool provided for him at the fire. He was given a hot cup of ale, a plate of steaming stew and some fresh fruit. He couldn't talk but noticed that Lazarus was seated beside him his pipe and tankard at hand. They had a bed and small tent set up for Riel and he didn't even remember hitting the pillow.

Riel was staring into the fire the next morning, fingering Ridel's heart (the vial Liam gave him of his mother's blood.) He was thinking about Astar and Mini. He would never see either of them again. Riel abruptly stood up. "OH MY GOD! How could I forget the vial?"

He started pacing back and forth. "Stupid, stupid me! I forgot about it! I can't believe I did this!"

Uriel could not understand what was going on. But since this was his sixth plate of fruit and berries, a light snack for a bear, he stopped eating long enough to say, "exactly what are you talking about?"

Riel ran to his saddle bag and tenderly retrieved Mini's tiny body which had become stiff. The Sloven had gathered around. He carefully laid her on a boulder by the fire. Dried blood covered her whole chest and face. He got out the vial and praying let a single drop of blood fall into her open mouth.

Lazarus said, "She is long dead Riel, and even now the flies are attracted to her, we had better bury her here before the wild animals want her bones."

"I am not sure if this is going to work, but Liam gave me this vial," said Riel. "Liam said it would heal if I remembered right, but I know she is dead. Perhaps I have wasted this drop or should have put all of it on her.

"If only if I had thought of it when she was shot, and I could have saved her."

Lazarus was moved to tears, and they dripped down his face and onto his jacket. "You know half of these plans were hers. We will put a monument and bury her here for you Riel. None of us will ever forget her name."

"No, Lazarus. I just don't know if I need to put more of the blood on her or if this is a total waste," said Riel. "No one and nothing have been resurrected from the dead, especially when flies are ready to feast on her. I just know I trust Liam and he gave me this for a reason."

"Well, take the middle road and put a second drop on her and save the last for someone else. That is what she would tell you to do," said Lazarus.

Riel decided that was going to be his course of action. He took the vial, uncorked it, raised to the sky, and said, "Lord we do this in your name, in the name of your Father and the Holy Spirit. If it is in your will, bring our sweet tiny Mini back from the dead. If it is not your will, then we will bury her in the new land and build an altar to honor your Holy name. We give you this decision. We pray for the exodus and the Sloven people, that you protect us all. Amen."

He kneeled and directed a second drop into Mini's heart wound. They waited an hour, but nothing happened.

The Sloven started to weep because Riel was bent over the Mini, sobbing. He stood up and said, "Enough, we have to move and quickly." He went to his horse and prepared to leave. He was about to retrieve Mini's body when Lazarus started shouting. "Riel, look, look!"

Twinkling gold light was descending from the sky onto the Mini's body.

It coalesced into bright vortex, formed an arrow of light and shot into Mini's heart wound.

Knowing light always had something to do with Liam, an hour later Riel ordered the Sloven to go on ahead while he, Lazarus, Uriel and Windring remained behind. Mini had not moved and remained dead. Uriel had consumed a dozen more plates of food and was lying beside the rock that contained Mini's now smelling body.

His paws were quivering, and he was sleeping on his back. He was dreaming about romping in a meadow with Fammy.

Suddenly the boulder just split in half and Mini disappeared in the cloud of debris. Uriel did not even flinch and continued snoring. Lazarus walked up and kicked the sleeping bear on his side. With one paw Uriel tossed Lazarus twenty feet into the air. Lazarus screamed all the way up and all the way down, but Uriel caught the frightened Sloven in his paws before he hit the ground. "I would NOT suggest you ever kick what appears to be sleeping bear. It is a dangerous business and are very lucky I consider you a friend. I am hungry again, but I've decided to let you live and see if I can catch up to the Sloven who left earlier for a fruit snack, not a Sloven snack."

Lazarus climbed down from the bear's paws and staggered off a few feet and then collapsed on the ground. He held his chest. "That was enough to give one a heart attack. I only wanted to find out what happened to Mini's body, Bear. I thought you were my friend." He was still breathing hard from the encounter.

Riel said, "Where is Mini?"

Mini popped her head out of Riel's pocket and said, "I personally think she was full of joy walking in the fields of Heaven with Liam when she was told that she had to come back down here and save your sorry asses. Excuse my French. Then she was back in her body and the boulder split in half below her."

Riel looked down in fright for a second and then realized Mini had taken up residence in her favorite pocket. Lazarus jumped in the air, but Uriel stood up and lumbered over Mini. "You are alive MIni! You were dead! My God! Liam has sent you back to us! Well, come to think of it, these guys are a hopeless mess without you." Uriel carefully rubbed his giant nose against Mini's tiny face as she was standing in Riel's pocket.

Riel reached down and brought Mini out of his pocket and set her back on the half boulder. "Forgive me for forgetting Ridel's Heart and not using the vial, leaving you dead for so long. If I had not been set on killing the General and so distracted because you died in my hands, I might have been thinking clearly. But you are here with us now. Thank you, Lord, for returning her to us."

"My idea of having a good time is not being here on this this very dim planet trying to get everyone moving," said Mini. "I was walking with Liam on the flowered meadows of Atislan about to meet those who have died before me when Liam explained that I needed to make a choice: Liam said 'Riel has twice dropped his mother's blood from Ridel's heart on your body. I will leave it up to you if you wish to return or not. There are consequences and you will feel some pain if you return, and it will not be pleasant after being here with me.' I thought about it but realized you are a totally lost and can hardly function without me. So here I am and believe me this most unpleasant, I am starving, thirsty and my chest hurts. Where are we and what has happened?"

"Most of the Sloven have crossed the River Chebar ahead of us a mile or so. The end of the Exodus is in front of us. We few waited on Riel, but he is hours late and your slow resurrection has delayed us too," replied Lazarus.

Uriel interjected, "Well I'm hungry and thirsty too. Let's get a quick meal and head out from here and catch up!"

Hours later, the King and his minions straggled into the Citadel. The people in the Citadel were not much better off as most of them had terrific headaches, a few were throwing up but all of them were staggering. Someone had opened the Lyon's gate as the Sloven were essentially out of the bag. They had to get water from the pit below as the whole cistern had to be emptied and no one knew what to do to get food. It was utter chaos with a host of complaints without the Sloven to help them.

The Scouts soon found the General's body in the pit and called for the King. Kester stood beside Enginele looking down, "So they have murdered my General on top of everything else! Tomorrow, we ride, and they will pay dearly for all of it! We will shred every Sloven child under 12 to pieces.

"Break out the war gear and prepare. Lieutenant you are now the General. Get the troops fed and ready, we leave at dawn!"

Commands and reality are two different things. As hard as Lieutenant Samuel, now General, tried, the men were tired and hungry.

The horses were exhausted and not well cared for after the bear escapade. Now there was no one in the stable, no servants in the kitchens, baths, salons, or apartments. Nothing was working right. Finally, someone figured out they would have to open the valve at the bottom of the cistern and drain the contents. It began to refill but, in the meantime, all of them had to go down to the pit to get water. Food was another story: At least there was still some fresh fruit and stale bread and buns, but no one knew how to start the ovens and stoves. General Samuel got a few of the officers to take care of the horses and some of his family to prepare food.

The next day, as centered as the Elegant were on returning their slaves, the troops were not able to leave until mid-morning. The King, still in a rage, stomped around issuing useless orders and demanded they leave immediately.

Finally, they exited the stables, the King in his regalia (of course) took the lead of his troops. Judging from the amount of discarded material on the road, the Sloven Exodus had much greater numbers than anyone knew about.

The King, glad to be moving, had to pay attention to the obstacles in the road. He did not notice the activity taking place behind in the Pit as Astar and a number of Elegant families prepared to follow the troops to war.

Riel, Mini, Uriel and Lazarus crossed the River Chebar and followed the stragglers trail.

The Sloven were not far ahead, but at least all the Sloven were now across the River Chebar and moving. Riel knew that the King was probably back at the Citadel by now, hot with rage and it would not be long before he would get his troops moving. Still the King's men were all mounted and could move fast. On the other hand, his small group of travelers could move even faster so he suggested an early finish to the day and that they rest and recover.

Everyone agreed, so Riel went to do his evening prayers. He was kneeling, his head bowed when Liam suddenly appeared. "Riel, I love you. You are my child. Stand and walk with me and I will explain what you must do now."

Riel Returned to the camp, just as a hot meal was being served. He was very tired, but he knew he had to tell the others their part in Liam's plan. They had just finished eating when Lawrence and Fammy and several Sloven back tracked and ran into the camp.

The joy and elation for the reunion lifted all of them.

When the hugs and tears were finished, Riel stood in the middle of them all and said, "Uriel, Fammy, Mini and Lawrence all must stay here. Lazarus will accompany me until I send him back to catch up with you. All the rest of you must move on and get the Sloven line moving as quickly as possible." Then he explained what he had to do. Lazarus was happy to stay behind until he learned he was going to be sent back halfway through.

Lazarus started yelling, "What are you talking about? You and our friends will all be killed. What a crazy, strange plan! Do you think the Elegant would ever respond? I can't believe you want to do this."

Riel calmly watched the Sloven stomping his feet and knew sending him back halfway hurt his feelings. "Lazarus, Liam has commanded this. I saw him a few minutes ago. If I go to my death, all the gain for me is just being with him. But I have been commanded and so have you."

"Liam? Where is He, I have never seen Him!" The Sloven looked around covering his eyes.

"Trust me, Lazarus, and trust in the Lord's plan," said Riel. "I will tell you all a parable: Once there was a great King and he told his General he was sending him out to war to represent his Kingdom. The King said, 'I want you to walk, straight, stand tall, and go and face the enemy but you must go with only the four I have assigned. With you goes my mighty name and the hopes and dreams of your people. You may see death in this but if only you step forward with faith and hope, then mighty things will be done in my name.'

"The General went to get his horse and a quick meal with the men he had served with. They all stood around with sad, grieving looks full of defeat for the five. The General stood up in front of them and said, 'I go to hold the standard and blessing for our people. I stand in the gap, and I go forth with conviction and strength in my heart. If you cannot celebrate with me, then turn to your sorrows and leave me to my meal. For I know I believe in our King and am persuaded I can hold his promises in stone. Great is our King and greatly to be praised.'"

The understanding dawned on Lazarus that Riel trusted the Lord with every fibre of his being and he would be obedient even if it cost him his life. They all bedded down for the night. The next morning was a sad separation with the Sloven going one way except for Lazarus and the others heading back to the River Chebar.

13

RIVER CHEBAR

"This is the living creature that I saw under the God of Israel by the river Chebar; and I knew that they were cherubim."
Ezekiel 10:20

The King, finally free of the obstructions on the road, spurred his midnight black horse setting a pace that some of the men could not compete with. The Lieutenant-General Samuel caught up and told the King he was putting himself in grave danger again being so far ahead.

Hours later, they were well organized by General Samuel, and they made the River Chebar.

However, evening was upon them, and they made camp.

The compadres all looked around at each other, their food cooling on their laps.

Mini said, "We cannot exactly celebrate but all of us are here now together, and we can eat this scrumptious breakfast and look at trees and mountains in the distance celebrating God's beauty." The Bears could only smell tinges of autumn in the air, having poor eyesight. Looking up, Lawrence, Mini and Riel all looked at the patches of gold, copper and amber near tree line. Soon fall would color the slopes. It was beautiful and they all spent a moment in reverie. Then they had to break camp.

Mini went up the front of Riel's jacket and settled on his shoulder. "Riel, I see the courage you had earlier is starting to slip away. Do not let the enemy take charge of your heart. I know you were born for this day and so do you. What do we need to do now?"

"I must bathe, oh dear, and be anointed and then dressed in my Ephod," said Riel. "I wonder where we can find water and some oil. I haven't seen anything since the River Chebar."

"There is water, but we must backtrack. We can use the cooking olive oil in your saddlebags," said Mini. "With you on Lawrence and me on Uriel it should not take long to get back there."

An hour later Mini told them to go right off the path onto an animal trail. The followed the tiny path through some heavy brush and emerged on a small stream with a wide pool.

It was deep in the center, just like a bathtub. Riel undressed while Lawrence turned around so Lazarus could get into the saddlebags and pack. Carefully Lazarus unloaded the priestly robes paying special attention to the many jewels on the garments.

Riel's teeth began to chatter in the cold mountain stream. Lazarus grabbed Riel's hand as he began to wash his hair. "I have brought a specially scented shampoo which I use on Astar's hair. If I can spend hours doing her hair, I can give you a coif."

Lawrence said, "Hey if you take all this stuff off my back, I might be able to reconnoiter back at the River Chebar and see what is going on while you do hair and get the getup on. You know, put on the fancy threads. Do up the do."

Riel completed his bath and Lazarus got oil and towels from his horse. Riel sat down on a nearby rock. Lazarus tied Riel's hair in several fine braids which he grouped into a gold band at the top of his head. Riel's face was now striking with his wide almond shaped eyes a dominate feature. Mini gasped when she saw him, "Oh my, oh my! You have matured: You have the face of a King."

"Lawrence, that is a good idea. It's not far back and you can come back and report as soon as possible. But Lawrence, remember you're much bigger and not brown anymore. You need to be careful in your striped Donkey tuxedo. Promise me." Riel smiled as he said this.

Lazarus took everything off Lawrence.

"Stealth is the name of my game!" Lawrence shifted his eyes back and forth and crouched down, attempting to freeze-move in stealthy starts and stops. He did not make a good cat. Then he took off in a dusty cloud.

Lazarus anointed Riel with the olive oil. "I, Lazarus of the Sloven, anoint you in the name of God, in the presence of Uriel, Fammy and Mini as our mighty sovereign, King of the Elegant and the Sloven, ruler of this land and others beyond our borders as Liam has said. Today you fulfill your destiny and become a Priest-King." Lazarus spilled the entire jug of oil over the top of Riel's head and the animals all bowed to the ground and praised God.

Lazarus helped Riel dress by standing on the top of a rock, assisting by carefully putting the white robe over the top of Riel's head. Then Lazarus placed the Ephod over that. Riel put on his cape, the crown on his head and picked up the scepter.

Lazarus saw Lawrence returning through the forest. He looked a little lost and was about to turn in the wrong direction. He was mumbling to himself, "I just can't believe it. The whole Citadel has emptied, and they are staged to cross the River Chebar! How do I tell Riel he is facing hopeless odds. I know they will kill me if only for my handsome self. Dear God and to think that Riel is back here having his hair done."

"We are over here," shouted Lazarus. Lawrence jumped but recovered enough to act like he was going in the right direction. He ran the last few feet.

"You are just so hard on your Donkey Riel." Lawrence collapsed on the ground in a heap, puffing up the dust. "What are you doing Riel? Us five are never going to succeed. You going to hit the buggers with a rock? You going to spit in their faces while they flay your guts?"

"I'm ready to be murdered if you wish, but not sure if I can maintain consciousness if they begin to torture you or anyone else. They are a brutal group! DO YOU realize what they will do with a handsome black and white Donkey? NO! NO! I can't bear thinking about their uses for me and my skin. I am feeling faint." Lawrence flipped over, put his hoofs high in the air and started trembling. "You may as well slit my throat right here and now!" He offered his neck as a token gesture.

Lazarus asked Riel, "Does the Donkey always act like this? He is very dramatic!"

Riel said, "He certainly is one of a kind." He was laughing out loud. "Please, kindly flip over Lawrence and tell us what is going on at the River Chebar."

A few minutes later Lazarus saddled Lawrence but left the saddlebags near the creek.

Riel mounted and draped his cape over Lawrence's back. The sun made the Ephod jewels flicker with light but the man in the saddle was the true star.

Lazarus stood in front of Windring holding his reins. He walked to the assembled group. "Well Riel, no matter the outcome today, you are my friend and will always be the king of my heart. Goodbye my good hearts, hopefully we will meet up again." A huge tear slipped down his face as he bowed before Lawrence, Uriel, Fammy and Mini. Lazarus turned and slowly walked back to Windring, hopped up on the saddle and rode out. Riel turned Lawrence to the River Chebar.

Lawrence set a good pace and started to sing halfway back:

Woe is me! Woe is me!
I am sacrificed at the hand of man.

Woe is me! Woe is me!
I am black and white, fitted with many stripes,
At Liam's hand I was changed overnight.
But I must go and fight, fight, Fight!

Woe is me! Woe is me!
No womenfolk will I ever smoke with my handsome self.
For I go to my slaughter without drink or fodder.

Woe is me! Woe is me!

At this, Lawrence began to blubber in earnest. Riel halted him in the path.

He got off and came around to look in Lawrence's face. "You seem to think this involves your death today? You know not once has Liam ever let us down. If we end up dying today, think about the places you have gone and you are the only Donkey to cross the Gates of Paradise."

"Was it that bad?" Riel asked. "Or do you think maybe Liam has a plan to let us live today and tomorrow? Whatever happens we will face this together and with dignity. You sing anything more like that and I am walking the rest of the way or riding Fammy."

"But look at me, I am young and handsome beyond words." Lawrence shifted so Riel had a side view and elongated his neck. "It's just not fair I am going to get slaughtered."

"You know Lawrence, it is not fair that I love Astar and she will likely kill me at her first opportunity," said Riel. "It is not fair I spent the whole summer with the crazy Elegant who think they are God's only chosen people. Now I face them as their mortal enemy and some of them became friends over the summer. I love you Lawrence as you always bring freshness and comedy to situations. You need to decide: Are you going with me today on the field of battle? I chose you over Windring. You are the one I brought with me!"

"I was your first choice? You, the King, chose me?"

"Yes, because I know you, you will do what I ask even if you do die," said Riel. "And yes, I am the anointed King and I know the Lord has even bigger things to conquer ahead for us."

"I am your choice! Wowser and hee haw!" said Lawrence. "Maybe I will make someone a nice coat. It will probably be Astar. I can just see her now showing off my beautiful hide to Elene and all the others. Hey, wait, why are you stopping when we could be racing on?" At this, Lawrence showed his large front teeth.

Riel could not help but laugh. He re-mounted Lawrence and picked up the pace.

They approached the River Chebar cautiously and Riel got off and led Lawrence along then left him in the bushes as he scouted ahead. The Elegant were like a hive of irritated yellow jackets but behind them a confusing cloud of dust rose high into the air. He walked back to the animals. "Well, this is it and we soon will be visible. I see the rock we are to stand on." Riel got his sword, swished in the air, and then sheathed it on his hip. He held his scepter in his hand. "Come on friends let's go do this or die."

14

FROM CHAOS

*"He that believes on me from him
shall flow rivers of living water."*
John 7:38

Back, the morning before Riel had crossed the River Chebar, the Elegant had just got the horses ready and packed up the camp, a real accomplishment considering they no longer had a single slave. The King, furious at the long delay, could not go forward without his troops. He was pacing back and forth under the trees at the back of the camp, a grim unsettled look on his face. Meanwhile, many of the Elegant who followed the troops had managed to catch up during the morning. All of them were choking on the road dust they had stirred up. Included in the mix were Astar, Elene and many other families. Some were very hungry and all of them thirsty and so further delayed the soldiers. A number them fell into the River Chebar on arrival, glad for the water, and then went in search of food. They visited anyone related and proffered food. The result was obvious: The soldiers did not leave their family members starving or hungry and the camp did not break until late in the morning.

Riel and the entourage found an easy way up the back of a huge, flattened boulder and climbed to the top. They were visible for miles standing in the blazing sun. If the archers wanted to shoot them with arrows, they most certainly were in range. The River Chebar was shallow and easy to cross in the waist deep water even on foot. Riel knew that the way he was dressed he couldn't be missed.

Riel stood there a few seconds when two of the Elegant scouts sounded their horns in alarm. Horses lined the opposite riverbank, but King Kester was left at the back of the camp unable to see what caused the commotion. He was not happy when he had to have his personal guard move several people and horses out of his way. When he got to the river's edge and cleared a space around him, he spotted Riel all decked out like some sort of priest-king standing as bold as brass within arrow range.

"So, you sneaking coward fleabag pig that tells nothing but lies, we meet as mortal enemies at last. You fooled us all with your whip when all along you deprive us of what is rightfully ours," yelled King Kester across to the boulder the companions were standing on.

"I am no coward Kester," said Riel. "I simply stopped you and the Elegant from murdering, using, and hurting the Sloven. I have named them 'Freemen' on this very day."

The King, during this exchange, whispered orders to General Samuel who ran off in haste.

"Are you saying the worthless traitor Sloven are calling themselves 'Freemen'? Oh, that is rich and ripe! Ha, ha, ha, ha, ha. I will see about that," replied the furious, ballistic ruler. Twenty archers lined up on the bank and prepared to fire.

"You have sacrificed your life and those of your animals for nothing. Why waste your lives on the useless, pathetic Sloven? We will catch those ungrateful pigs and after torturing and murdering half of them, we will put the rest in cages. You can do nothing to stop us now. You fooled all of us except my daughter. She was suspicious of you from the start and after you used her shamelessly. However, before we shoot you and those animals down, I am curious about your clothing. It is so beautiful; I am going to enjoy wearing it when you are dead. We will torture you, then disembowel you, cut off your head and hang it above the Lyon's Gate. Still, I would like to know where it came from. The jewels on the front are especially interesting." The King squinted in the morning sun and covered his eyes.

"Liam gave it to me in Paradise, King Kester," Riel's eyebrow raised as he said this.

"Liam," Kester laughed. "When could you, as a lying disgusting traitor, have met him whom the Elegant have aways served?"

"I have more than met him, Kester, he covered me at the Gates of Paradise, and we crossed into Heaven," said Riel. "Liam gave me this king and priest clothing and He is here with us now and you are found judged and wanting. There is not even one of us who can measure up to His glory, mercy, or grace. I know I purposely deceived you, but I never once lied to you.

"For any deception I committed, I ask your forgiveness."

All the Elegant laughed at this. This went on for a moment and then Kester said, "So Liam chooses liars and cheats to cover and fulfill a prophecy more than 1,000 years old. Surely you see absurdity of your tale. I think this is just a delay tactic." Kester just then, realized that the animals at Riel's side were part of the Prophecy and the two bears were exceedingly rare.

"You have kept, murdered, enslaved, tortured, and kept the Freemen for over 400 years," said Riel. "They are God's people too and Liam has had enough of your false praise, arrogance, and hypocrisy. He sent me to free them and I stand between you and them. Your people are nothing but blind, lazy, overbearing murderers. I tried to talk to you about the Lord's ways, but you never heard a word. Today you will hear them."

Kester's anger erupted unchecked, "Aim at his heart and fire."

Astar screamed and cried out, "Father do not kill him." The arrows, shot in unison, were already in the air. They arched above the River Chebar, knocked into an invisible wall, and felt into the water. The archers looked at each other and reloaded.

Riel moved towards them across the rock as his face began to glow and the animals followed. His eyes were coals of hot burning fire. Lawrence stood beside Riel.

Lawrence exclaimed, "I wouldn't be aiming your arrows at King Riel Ran Agam! The angels from the Gates of Paradise are standing in his defense in the middle of the River Chebar. Liam is defending us! Yippee!"

"That Donkey is talking! I don't believe it," said General Samuel.

"Look, look there is the black and white, striped donkey in that painting," said someone in the crowd. "He's talking and there are two, not one Filk bears! That's in the painting too! There is the funny animal on top of one of the bear's head." A shudder ran through the crowd as some realized that they might be facing the real thing.

Kester smiled at the deception his people started to believe. He was smarter than that. "You expect us to believe that Liam and his angels are defending you when you are simply doing a few little magic tricks? None of us are so stupid to believe that. You think making it look like the Donkey can talk scares me? I don't think so!" He turned and gave commands to General Samuel.

"Before you command and commit to this, Kester," said Riel. "I warn you that I also see what Lawrence sees. Death is standing in the River Chebar, waiting for the men you just commanded to kill me. He is young and vibrant as many will walk his way today at your command."

A band of men charged the River Chebar, swords, and spears at ready. They galloped their horses hard on into the water shouting, "Death to all who would oppose the Elegant." A moment later they ran into the angel's granite skirts and came to a sudden halt. Some looked skyward as the Angel's spears rained down on them. A second later lightning shot through them all as the biting, bone-vibrating screams shocked everyone on the shore.

There was smoke coming out of the mens, ears, mouths and noses as their bodies began to disintegrate. Their flesh became ashes and their skeletons dropped from their shrieking horses. The swords and spears in their hands fell to earth and the horses ran downstream in utter panic.

"You alone are responsible for the death of those men Kester," Riel said. "I am crying out to you Elegant in this wilderness. You have murdered and maimed in the name of our Lord Liam. I call you to repentance. Come and all who would lay down their arms, repent of evil and follow our true King and Savior, Lord Liam. I have been anointed this very day to lead you. Do not be deceived for I am just a man like you, but I am Liam's man heart and soul. Come to me and cross the River Chebar. If your hearts are true, you will cross unharmed. If you come, I promise you that although life will not be easy, you will step into Paradise for eternity."

Both bears stood on their hind legs and said in unison, "What King Riel says is true." They went back down on all fours and bowed their heads to the ground. Lawrence and Mini also bowed except Mini was hard pressed to hang on to Uriel's ears and almost tumbled forward when he bowed.

"A pretty speech that was! It is you using evil to kill my men," commented Kester. He did not see his daughter Astar leading her horse, both Mathematicians and several others wading out into the water. A moment later everyone realized what they intended.

The King, livid and even more enraged, said, "What? You betray your own people?"

Elgenius turned around and answered the King, "We have known for many years the only real mathematicians are the Sloven. We pretended to know what we were doing but we only used their minds and unfortunately some of their bodies. When Riel says we will walk with him in Paradise we believe him. Look at the Donkey, he has black and white stripes, and he can talk. The bears talk and are the biggest beasts we have ever heard of, and the male has a golden collar and hump just like in the painting. We are tired of the lies. We are crossing over to Riel no matter the cost."

Kester was at a complete loss of words for a few seconds as others joined them in the River Chebar.

"Astar, you the most corrupt murderer of all and killer of your children, you cannot do this," exclaimed Riel worry crossing his face. "Unless you are true and repented, the angels will strike you down and you will go to hell this very day. If you doubt cross back to your Father."

Astar looked at Riel above her and said, "I had not lived until the day you took the whip from my hand. I knew all along that you were not the man you appeared to be but something much more. I knew some great destiny was in your future."

"I promise you nothing Astar, regarding our relationship," said Riel. "I have much more work to do for Liam and you cannot be any part of that. You will have to stay with the Freemen and they hate you with good cause."

"I am still coming," said Astar.

By this time the two Mathematicians had duck waddled out to the Angel's skirts. Their long pink hat feathers were soaked and stuck to their stately red garments. Etharis, the largest and most ungainly of the two, had slipped and Elgenius tried to keep him upright.

Both took a dip. Dripping they both closed their eyes, held each other's hands, and stepped through the translucent barrier and waded to the other shore. Surprised and filled with joy, they tried to jump in the air unsuccessfully. Then they searched until they found a way up to Riel and kneeled, soaking wet at his feet like two huge, sunbaked hippos.

Astar continued to advance but Riel pointed and stopped her. "Astar, stop and get off your horse. Take all your jewelry, your beads and gold off. Oh yes and the knife. You must walk through if you are coming."

She stopped almost mid-river and said to her father, "For good or for worse, I love you Father, but I must follow my real King. I have never loved any other man besides him. But of all my friends and lovers, there is no one compared with Riel. It is time for me to make this decision and I choose to repent. I can still see my babies faces every time I go to bed at night. I cannot continue the way I have been living and I choose Riel even if it costs me my life."

By this time a huge group of the Elegant had dropped their gold, jewels, weapons, and feathers and waded into the water. A few of them were the king's personal guard. They also safely made the passage across.

Riel called out, "Repent and walk into the water if you want eternal life with Liam. Do not let your hard-hearted King dissuade you from being God's person."

Kester ordered his soldiers to follow and kill as many as they could who had crossed or were in the River Chebar. Two of the soldiers charged ahead and were met with the same results as the first group; their flesh gone and skeletons smoldering in the water, their horses screaming and running downstream. The rest of the people stopped in the water looking first at King Kester and then to King Riel. Then, some more of the Elegant waded into the water.

General Samuel was almost at the center of the River Chebar when he suddenly threw his lance. It hit the Angel's barrier, busted in half, and bounced back into the water. Taking this as his final cue, he stepped down off his horse, took off his sword, feather, armor, and gold chains and threw them back towards Kester. Then he stepped across the shimmering gap and went to Riel where he got down on his knees and bowed. By this time, it was getting crowded on the rock. Some of them were prostrate but most were on their knees.

Riel moved to the rock edge by the River Chebar and said, "This is my last call. Any others who would come, enter the River Chebar, and pass through. Behold what stands in defense of me." He raised his scepter and swirling mist formed on the water, it soon coated the angels, and they became more translucently visible. A few more women and young men threw off their valuables and waded into the water. A moment later the angels began to build a wall. The final few passed through just as the final gap in the wall closed.

Suddenly, terror gripped the Elegant and the horses began to buck and run. King Kester managed to stay on his horse, but his heart was filled with sorrow for the loss of his daughter and people. He turned around to see smiling, black-robed Death grabbing a young man who had been tossed off his horse, landing on his head. Unfortunately, then his horse landed on top of him. Death smiled at Kester and said, "You should have repented and crossed to Riel too. Many of your people would have followed your lead, but now you have chosen misery and your own people will hate you. Then I will come again but I will not take you to Paradise." Death laughed causing Kester to cover his ears and cringe as his body felt the cold breath as the thing's spirit pass by him. Others were not so lucky, Death gathered them and disappeared.

Riel shouted, "King Kester, from this day forward this river is closed to you and anyone who stayed behind. There is a great wall between the Elegant and Freemen that cannot be crossed. Anyone responsible for holding the Freemen will not cross without dying from this generation and the next."

15

HOMEWARD BOUND

"The he said unto him, come home with me and eat bread."
I Kings 13:15

Riel assembled the people a mile away under a huge spreading green oak tree. Many were already tired, hungry, and thirsty.

"What are we going to do now, Riel? These people are used to having servants and they are already hungry and tired. Look at the Mathematicians they are so fat they just dragged their enormous derrières into camp, and we have only walked a mile. Look at Astar, she's all wilty, frazzled and exhausted. We have hundreds of miles to go." Lawrence let out a moan and looked at the earnest faces facing Riel.

Uriel said, "I am not taking them two corpulent, chunky, full-buttocks, broad in the beam, scholars on my back."

Riel turned to Uriel and glared at him. "Really Uriel!"

"I ain't taking them either. I must preserve my vertebrae," said Lawrence his tail riding high in the air.

"I ain't a gonna do it Riel, even if you asked me to! Final decision," replied Uriel.

Riel put his hand to his head in frustration and said, "Well this is a mess, so I think it is time to pray. All of us." The Elegant mostly dropped to their dirty knees and bowed their head. The two scholars tried but ended up sitting on a nearby rock instead. Lawrence and Fammy, and Uriel went down on their haunches.

"Lord, Liam these people have repented. Many of them have committed unspeakable crimes." Riel opened his eyes and dropped a quick gaze at Astar. She was the only person prostrate on the ground near the crowd edge. "Lord, in your kindness and mercy you allowed these souls to cross the River Chebar. Now we are in the wilderness and have no means of shelter or support. Please, give me wisdom to know what to do. We do not know your intent or purpose in leading us to here, but we step forward in faith, trusting in your mercy and abundance to sustain us. Be with us and guide us forward. Amen."

Together everyone whispered, "Amen!"

Riel had the people rest while he consulted with the animals and was particularly interested in Mini's take on this desperate situation.

"I sure hope you got some big, wise, religious, and worthy plan or suggestion Riel because your Donkey is clean out of ideas. Perhaps we will lead these people to their deaths taking them to the Sloven, excuse me, 'Freemen' who hate their guts," remarked Lawrence.

"Now listen, these people have repented and need to be encouraged, not reminded about their past or the shape of their bodies Uriel and Lawrence." Riel looked at the Uriel and Lawrence until they both hung their heads.

"Riel, you know that stream you bathed in this morning? I can smell it on the wind. We need to get them water first. It is not that far, and I think if we can do it with a few rest stops. They can make it except for the two scholars. Look at them," injected Mini.

All of them turned and viewed the two men who were in a heap collapsed together. It was a sorry sight as the dye in their hats and clothes dripped down their faces and stained their hands. Dirt added to the picture of calamity.

"Well Mini has a good idea, Riel. I can smell water too. But I got news, I don't think this group is going to make it that far. And remember I am final on the fatsos." Lawrence swished his tail back and forth.

"I think that's what we should do, Mini. It's not that far but you three must help the Mathematicians, if we need to, we can build a travois and you three can pull it. You must encourage those men they were one of the first and encouraged many others," Riel answered. He gave a hard look at Lawrence but this time the Donkey met his gaze and would not look down.

"FAT chance," said Uriel. Lawrence laughed.

All of them rested for an hour and the heat of the day passed and the afternoon sun dipped lower in the sky.

Riel announced, "It's time to move on. There is a cool stream ahead of us. You will need to walk as far as you can and then stop to rest for a few minutes. Lawrence will lead us, and the bears and I will bring up the rear. We can help with the last in line."

Longing eyes rested on Riel and one woman said, "You told us to put everything down or throw it back on shore. We can't even hunt we have no weapons or arrows. But more than that, we have no horses."

"You have been stripped of your earthly goods for a reason: Faith is based on things hoped for, not things that you feel and see. You are going to have to trust Liam and me," replied Riel.

No sooner had Riel said this than a flash of light burst in a distant copse of trees. A figure walked beneath.

The two scholars got up and started to run towards the trees but slowed to a walk a few feet later. "It's Liam, it's Liam! He is shining beneath those trees and signaling for us to go to him," they shouted. They managed most of the distance but Riel and Fammy had to assist the last hundred yards because they were totally out of breath and very hot.

They were elated until they found out Liam was gone.

When the group got there en masse, there were two very large furry buffalo and a whole herd of strangely tame and docile deer.

"What are we supposed to do now," inquired an on-looker.

Riel started laughing and said, "Well I suggest you get on your rides, and we should be to the creek shortly. You two get on those huge buffalo." He pointed at the beast, but the scholars were less than enthusiastic. Little did they know that premonition was utterly true.

Riel walked over to the beasts and overheard their conversation.

One buffalo said to the other, "Great! Good grief, do you see the size of those two men?"

"Liam asked us or there would be no way on this earth I would carry either one of those two. We've been buffaloed into giving houses a ride." At this point the Buffalo snickered as an evil plot passed silently between the two brothers. "We could return to the herd tonight if we hurry. It's not that far to the creek if the man things don't cripple us for life."

Riel said, "You two should be ashamed of yourself. What are your names?"

"I am Bully, and he is Billy. We didn't know a human could understand our speech."

"You must the King Liam told us about. Are you really expecting us to carry those two mountain-sized men?"

"I am King Riel Ran Agam. And yes, you must carry the two Elegant SCHOLARS who deserve your abidance and respect."

"He meant a-ridance... and ride spect," said Billy grinning with wide-white teeth, as only buffalos do. Their sense of word play is very developed in some of the older beasts.

Deep in thought Bully stared at Riel. "You know Billy, I think he really is the King in the Prophecy. I mean look at the outfit and crown. Look how his mane is fixed too, bet his fur is curly like ours. That is the mane or main reason I took up with Mottle my mate you know. Her fur and then I saw her running in this meadow filled with yellow flowers that have this tasty pepper flavor and a nice little crunch. Yummy!

"Hey ho, this man is a looker for a human. You know I bet we are the two buffalos in that story. Can you imagine when we return and tell everyone?"

Billy said, "I think it is the man his-self. No wonder Liam picked us two as we are the biggest, but we are not fat like the two humans. Wait until my mate Cow-Patti hears about this. My son will speak with reverence to me after this! I'm sure he is the King!"

Lawrence was intrigued listening to Riel let out two snuffs and a long sort of bellow. "I think he is talking to those two buffalos, Uriel. They don't really know how gigantic those two men are, or they would be running as fast as they can back to their herd." Lawrence snickered and Uriel joined him.

"Better than us two my friend," replied Uriel.

Riel looked at Bully and Billy and said, "Big is better and applies to buffalo too. Now go get those men and take them to the creek you can smell."

The two buffalo brothers watched Riel walk off and Bully said, "We can institute our plan and have fun being obedient. I am looking forward to it!"

The Elegant had mostly mounted the deer who looked resigned to this ultimate indignity of carrying people. It was Liam's command, so they did it without complaint.

Lawrence led the way as deer have very little vision and only perceive things that move. Distance sight for them is a real problem. Riel rode on Uriel at the back, watching the two buffalo who purposely headed for every rut, trough, furrow, cut, gouge, and channel they could find. Some of the routes a goodly distance from the herd of deer. There was a cacophony or moans, ouches, laments, cry, screams and tears from the two men on their backs. The group arrived at the creek just as the moon began to rise and the last of the sun shimmered over the distant mountains. It was a warm night and thick grass dotted the flowered meadow. Everyone stopped and had a long restorative drink from the creek.

"I don't think I can take another step until I get something to eat," said a tiny lady who looked like she might faint.

"I am sorry but tonight we all must fast," Riel answered, "There simply is only provision for a few. Perhaps if we pray together before we rest?"

The Mathematicians were the very last to arrive. The buffalo had taken a detour to go up and down a creek cut near the field's far edge. The two of them literally rolled the men off their backs and ran into the trees snorting and laughing the whole way. "Them two are not going to be walking anywhere tomorrow, Bully! There isn't an inch on them that is not bruised or hurting! This was more fun than I have had in ages."

Riel retrieved the food packs and got out a few journey cakes. He took one of them to the little lady and said, "I can give you a mouthful, but many will not even get that this night."

She looked at Riel's sweet face filled with compassion and said, "Yesterday I would have tried to rip that cake from your hand. I will not take it today even though I am hungrier than I ever have been in my whole life. Today I want you to give my portion to one of the children."

Riel went to the several children that has crossed with their parents. He prayed over the tiny cake and broke off the first piece handing it to the first little girl. When he got to the last young man, the cake was still the same size as when he started.

The boy's mother cried out, "The CAKE! THE CAKE! It is the same as when he started feeding the kids. It is a miracle. We have something to eat."

Riel broke off more and more pieces and the more he broke off the more he fed. Soon they were all full and the scholars, who had to have others attend them and drop pieces of food into their mouths because they were laying face up on the grass and couldn't move, complained bitterly that they had never hurt so bad, nor been so far in a single day.

They did look the part. Their expensive clothing was in shambles, ripped and torn as the dye was on everything after the water; their hats and feathers long gone, their faces, arms, hands, and feet were smeared with different colored dye and scratched and covered in dirt. Elgenius, who took the worst of it on Bully, had several twigs sticking out of his unkempt hair. It seems he had encountered a low tree and a larger bush the buffalo took delight in going through.

The two of them ate three times what everyone else did as compensation.

Riel mumbled to the animals, "I wonder what else has in store for these people? I hope they remember what Liam is doing for them."

"We will never forget Riel. I am a scribe and intend to write all of this down when I get my implements back. I left them back at the River Chebar," said one of the women. "Looking at the scholars laying out in the meadow, I don't believe I will include any mathematics in that text either. The one on the left looks particularly roughed up."

"What is your name?" inquired Riel.

"I am Miriam. I am ashamed to say I came along yesterday to watch my son and husband slaughter the Sloven. When I saw you standing on the rock and the arrows flying towards you, I thought, *I hope every single one of them goes right into your devious heart.* Then they fell into the water as though something was between us and you. Then I thought, *Wait a minute. He is only one single man, and we are God's chosen people, why can't we kill him?*

"Then your face began to glow, and your crown and jewels were sparkling. It finally dawned on me you were the man of the Prophecy. I couldn't grasp it for a few minutes. The more it sunk into my soul, the more trueness rang in my heart. I am deeply ashamed for I honestly believed that the Sloven… ahhhhh… 'Freemen' were meant to be our servants and were less than the rats that ran in the gutters. I have beaten them, abused them and had my husband murder one of the women because I believed she stole my mother's brooch.

"I found it some months later behind a piece of furniture and then my daughter admitted to me she was playing with it and lost it. I treated my dog better than I treated them. I attended every Church service, I helped the Elegant poor, and never lied or cheated.

"When you called us to repent, for the first time I heard a small still voice say in my head, *Repent Miriam, repent! Your deeds are as filthy rags in my sight.* Then incidents I have had with the Sloven began to replay in my mind. I could see the faces of some of their children when I denied them food. I played every mistake or incident and punished them severely for any transgression. I am a cruel horrible person, Riel. Then you called to us again and I heard the voice say, *I have great plans for you my daughter Miriam. You have a hope and future. Go now.* You were like a dazzling beacon and then I saw the translucent angels standing in the River Chebar. I dropped all my earthy goods there and waded into water.

"My husband and son stopped me and said, 'you will be burned, and your skeleton will be all we can bury.'" I just kept walking. By this time, you were so bright and full of light I could not even look at you. I now know what I must do, and I will not spend one more minute of my existence on religion that has nothing to do with a living God. I have seen the way and I will follow you and it for as long as I live."

Riel looked at her sweaty, dirty face and said, "Miriam, this is a day when I have hundreds of people who have walked and rode deer some miles. I am very tired. I need to pray and so do you. We need to be very careful to walk on the Lord's path and not our own. I have many sins also, but each day I pray for forgiveness and mercy. Then the dawn breaks and I find I am forgiven, His promises fresh and new, filled with mercy and grace towards us. Help me help your own people and you will be doing Liam's will."

"I will do whatever you may ask," Miriam picked up the edge of her robe and walked back to the fire. She helped some bed down for the night. She was particularly tender with the mathematicians bringing them sweet cut grass for pillows and covering one of them with her own robe. It did not cover much of him, but it did comfort him. Both were snoring before she even finished.

She looked up and realized how stunning the sweeping moonless night was with a golden headed comet, its iridescent bright green and blue tail winging across the soft blue clouds. It was balmy after the warm day and the smell of meadow grass sweetened her senses.

Riel was smiling at Miriam as she walked away. He walked over to the creek looking up at the comet and bright stars. Riel suddenly also became aware of the dazzling scene in front of him. He could just make out people sleeping under the trees and in the meadow, the bright comet staining the atmosphere with color. He turned around just as Astar came through the bushes. Her hair was a tangled mess, her face streaked with dirt and sweat, her fine clothes in tatters. He had never seen her look so beautiful. He walked towards her. She looked very tired.

"I am sorry Astar, I have not had time to talk to you today."

"I am just so overwhelmed with my past and the people I hurt, murdered and had tortured," said Astar. Two huge tears ran down her cheeks. "How could I think I had the right? How could I have had my own baby boy... ah ahhhhh head cut off?"

Then she started weeping in earnest drawing deep breaths between sobs.

"There is a huge difference between guilt and the conviction of the Holy Spirit, Astar.

"You were born into a sinful nature, just like I was," said Riel. "You made choices based on what you believed. Sin is sin and it has no degrees. It is all bad in the Lord's sight. Now that you know the truth, do your best to sin no more. Liam has set you free of your past and made you a new creature. Study his truth, know his words, connect with his wishes, and experience the grace He freely gives to us all."

"Oh... but... the babies... my babies... I sold them." She sobbed uncontrollably.

"Stop this Astar. Stop it! Liam has brought you through and you are here with us. You rode a deer for most of the afternoon and ate from one biscuit the size of my fist that feed all your people, two ravished bears, a marmot and one very stubborn and silly Donkey. Stop feeling sorry for yourself and start helping people."

She looked up with her long black lashes glistening with tears and said, "But Riel, I just don't know how."

"I want you to know something." Liam said. "Your past has consequences. I don't know what the Freemen are going to say when we arrive. I will stand for you and your people just like I stood for the Freemen at the River Chebar. You can start by finding Lawrence and bringing him to me."

A tiny smile crossed her lips as she scanned the trees and meadow for the Donkey.

Lawrence had accompanied her most of the day singing silly songs about silly things, talking non-stop about his need for fresh carrots. Her favorite subject was about crossing the breaks at Rippon Pass which was seared into his memory. It really comforted her listening to his banter.

Riel washed his face in the creek and removed his Ephod carefully folding it and putting it next to him where he bent down to pray. He went down on his knees, bent forward and putting his hands between the rock and his forehead began to pray in earnest. He mumbled a few words and fell fast asleep leaning on the rock.

"Would you look at that Astar! The poor boy is totally exhausted. He hasn't let up for three or four days running around before that with the hunt stuff. I know he was very scared when your father had him shot with all those arrows." Lawrence let out a deep sigh.

"Did you actually say he was scared?" She looked at the Donkey with total disbelief. "Oh, yes, he doesn't want to die just like the rest of us. He just knew he had to face your Father and his army. Liam told him to. When you shot the arrows, I saw Riel close his eyes in resignation, as surprised as you were when they fell into the water," said Lawrence.

"But he talked like he knew Liam would protect him! I don't understand. He was willing to be shot and die to protect the Sloven... no ah... Freemen?" Astar asked.

"NO, he talked to you all like he knew no matter what that he was in the place Liam wanted him to be. If the Lord required his life, Riel was willing to give it." said Lawrence.

"Yes, he was willing to die for what was right."

Astar looked at the man's sleeping face, such strength, conviction, and courage.

"Hey, let's make him a nice grass bed, put out his bed roll, take some of his clothes off along with those weird gold shoe thingies. Somehow, I don't think he's going to wake up much. The bears are on watch tonight, although I don't know what could attack us with the wall keeping the Elegant out. Would you help please?"

Astar helped Lawrence, although he did little except to assist with Riel staggering to his bed. They soon got him settled and covered with a blanket. He slept through almost all of it. Astar bedded down beside him and laid awake listening his deep breathing until she drifted off herself.

The next morning Riel was still asleep under the huge oak next to the creek.

Everyone took a wide berth not to disturb him, but they met near the campfire on the other side of the meadow. The main topic was food. Fammy and Mini took over trying to tell the Elegant how to survive.

A few groups were formed after Fammy told them how to find berries and eatable plants. Each animal took out one group. They agreed to meet back at noon. Uriel and his group found a huge berry patch so tangled no creature could enter except perhaps a mouse. The women hiked up their long robes making cloth bowls for the harvest. Working the perimeter, huge, red raspberries were ripe for the picking and soon everyone's lips were bright red and their teeth stained. Not the least of these was Uriel who relished the sweet juice. Lawrence found asparagus plants near the creek and tubers that only needed be cooked. They were fine raw for the likes of a Donkey.

Fammy found a patch of mysterious bushes covered in small seed. She tested some of the germ and remembered eating this plant when she was a cub. They were sweet as honey. Miriam placed a cloth that covered her head under the bush and shook it and a huge cloud of the seeds fell off. Soon the whole group had devised ways to catch the produce. Mini was left in camp with a few others to keep watch since Riel was still asleep, and their few possessions were left behind. They all returned to find that Mini had found rocks with inverted surface bowls that served as cooking pots when heated. She had her group set them up on four stones for legs and had them build fires underneath them. The biggest rock bowl she had them draw creek water and it was already boiling when everyone returned. She also had them construct a crude oven of sorts that maintained the heat from the fire below.

When everyone returned, they piled the bounty in the middle of camp and Mini and Lawrence taught them what to do to get a hard tack biscuit put together. They also had a nice asparagus and potato soup boiling. The others cleaned and prepared the rest. It was a happy productive group when Riel finally woke later in the afternoon.

Riel woke to find Astar sitting on a rock beside him with a hot biscuit, a cup of fresh creek water and a handful of raspberries. When his eyes opened, she dipped her hem in the creek and washed his face wiping it clean with her hair. Riel blinked and raised himself on one elbow surprised to realize it was late afternoon.

"I thought you didn't know what to do," said Riel.

"Lawrence told me what to do and then to sit here until you wake up. I didn't really wait long."

"What is that wonderful smell? What is Uriel doing over there?" Riel asked.

"Mini constructed an oven and we found these bushes covered in these delicious seeds. She told us how to make these cakes and they are incredible. They also have hot soup at the campfire," Astar replied.

"The bear is trying to sneak up nearer to the ovens because Fammy insisted he had to wait for everyone to eat before they gave him the leftovers. He is after the biscuits, and he's already eaten ten of them. I guess that's a snack for a bear of that size.

"Someone told me that he ate half of all the raspberries they picked too. I guess if anyone deserved that food it was him after the last few days."

Just then Uriel tried a maneuver to get his huge hulk closer to the rock where the biscuits lay cooling. His rear-end shimmied and rotated and then he rotated his front in the same direction. Astar burst out laughing. "As if no one is going to notice that huge thing shifting himself closer."

Uriel looked around with shifty eyes. He darted the last ten yards swooped up a biscuit pile and threw them in his mouth. He looked around sheepishly and returned to his previous position. Half of the biscuits had disappeared. Riel and Astar both laughed.

Riel got up, bathed, and put on his forest green clothes and went to the campfire for some soup. Astar went and found Mini and Lawrence and told them Riel was awake.

"I'm still hungry and I'd like a nice big chunk of meat. I don't like soup," complained one of the men. "I'd really like a carafe of wine and some sliced cheese and fresh bread like we always had in the Citadel. Maybe we've made a mistake here," said another woman.

Riel could not believe his ears. "You have an opportunity for eternity, and you are complaining over food already? Who said that? You got fresh food this morning when I didn't know what to do to feed all of you. Look at Uriel eating all those biscuits! They taste like honey, and you can see even a bear enjoys them." Uriel took that moment to flip over on his back and suck on a biscuit in sheer unadulterated pleasure. His eyes were closed, he had five or six biscuits in his paws, and he was laid out on the grass like an up-side- down blanket. Everyone just laughed.

Riel assembled his traveling cohorts in a circle beside the campfire. It was difficult because Uriel had not finished his biscuits.

"Okay. We have so many people and they are not used to traveling, making their own food, combing their own hair, or not being assisted. They did well this morning, but I don't think we should move them with so much food nearby. And I am worried about the water too as I know it's dry for the next hundred miles. Mini and Fammy do you think you could go find Lazarus and get some help? Maybe you need to take Lawrence with you to explain? Or should I just take Lawrence and go?" Riel said.

Fammy and Mini said, "Take Lawrence and go. We can hold the fort here and you need to explain to Lazarus." Mini added, "They will want to kill them all you know with good reason. You'll be lucky if they even agree to come back and get us."

"Well one way or another they are our responsibility. You seem to be doing well with them though and they are quick learners. I am going to go with Lawrence then if you all agree," said Riel.

"I think you need to take Mini with you. She spent the most time in the pit and I have a feeling they will need her there with the stragglers and last of the Freemen anyway," Fammy said.

"Okay! We are all agreed: Mini, Lawrence and I will go ahead and get help if we can. Fammy and Uriel stay behind and take care of our wards."

An hour later, Riel was mounted on Lawrence, Mini on Riel's lap, the saddle bags packed with food and supplies ready to go. The spare packs with the Ephod and other unnecessary things left behind.

The Elegant were now crowded into a group and some were unhappy Riel was leaving them. Some thought he was going ahead to return with the Sloven so they could murder them. Some even thought he was deserting them. However, it was only a few and the rest knew it was a necessary inconvenience.

Lawrence, of course, had to have his moment of glory and with tail raised high, he did a little dance with his hooves then pranced around circling the crowd twice yelling "Goodbye, I go with all alacrity to save your sorry butts. Your very own black and white esteemed messenger. A king of the Donkeys. Smart, intelligent, wise, fast, and reliable to the extreme. Your very own doer of good deeds. Helper to the redeemed Elegant! The ride for King Riel!"

"Will you get a grip Lawrence and leave please," Riel said.

For effect, the Donkey suddenly took off, leaving a dust cloud in his wake.

Riel, knowing Lawrence's sense of humor, was waiting for this, and had gripped the reins and put pressure on his knees.

However, that pace slowed considerably an hour later. Lawrence settled into a canter because he understood he would have to maintain for some distance. They rode all day, part of the evening, made camp and set off early the next day.

16

TRAVELERS

"He that believes on me
from him shall flow rivers of living water."
John 7:38

Even at the punishing pace Lawrence set, it took another day to get to the last of the Freemen. They were just entering Wolf Pass when Lazarus stepped out from behind a large bush. "It took you long enough to report back to us. We were going to send out a party to backtrack and see what happened to you."

"Well obviously, no need!" Riel got down off Lawrence and picked up Lazarus and swung him in the air and then hugged the little man.

Lazarus hugged Riel back and started to blubber. "We thought they might have killed you and all of us were so worried."

Riel set Lazarus down. "I need to council with you Lazarus. I brought Mini along to help you understand. We need to have you help us and return with us."

"Why? The bears can take care of themselves. I am confused you just got here," replied Lazarus looking up into Riel's face. Mini hopped over from Riel to Lazarus and sat on his shoulder.

Mini said, "Do you have members of the counsel you were talking about here with you now?"

"Not all, but three members. Why?"

"Well, we need to sit down, have some food and water and discuss something with you."

"Let me get the others to make food, you get settled and we will assemble all of us together. There are about 25 of us bringing up the rear and we hear the front is near our destination."

A few minutes after Riel had refreshed himself, the Freemen were all seated on a circle of rocks and talking among themselves. Riel, with Mini in his pocket, stood and addressed them all. "We have gathered you together in hope of you extending forgiveness and mercy. After you left us and we returned to the River Chebar, many of the Elegant repented of their wrongs and crossed the River Chebar. It was being guarded by four huge angels sent by Liam. King Kester ordered me killed and several the archers tried to shoot me, Fammy, Mini, Uriel and Lawrence. The Elegant could not see the angels guarding us but their arrows hit them mid-river and fell into the water. Then I explained to their people that they needed to repent and start a new life. Then the angels became translucent.

"The people needed to throw away their earthly valuables and cross the water to me. Meanwhile, King Kester had some of his men rush towards us only to be incinerated by lightning and their skeletons dropped into the River Chebar. But the people who repented, crossed through unharmed and we have them back at camp a few miles from the River Chebar. We need all of you. We got them all camped safely, near food and water but we can never get them to you in their Elegant, helpless state. This is a wilderness in many ways to them. You must take them in and treat them as your own."

The Freemen were frozen in a sort of horrid stupor. Then suddenly all of them started talking.

Lazarus, the loudest and most angry of them all, shouted, "Our own? OUR OWN! Those murdering thieves that took our lives away? They killed our children for God sakes! They treated us as less than dogs or rats! No. No. NO! NO! NO!!!!!!!!"

Lazarus was hopping around, his face fueled red with fury, flinging his arms.

Riel waited until everyone had quieted and said, "Did I not stand and face the arrows and a whole army on your behalf when I am not one of you? Did I not show you mercy and grace, did I not give you this opportunity to be free?"

Mini hopped up to Riel's shoulder and stood on her hind legs. "Do you think maybe this is Liam's doing and by his command?" exclaimed Mini. "We came to get you and you must think about all the time I spent helping you, preparing you for this journey. The whole summer really and I am just a Marmot who left her mountain home because I was needed. You think your people have been kind to us animals? No, you have not. Humans and Sloven shoot, maim, and murder us at every turn. Yet I helped you. I traveled many miles with you and gave you ways to move your old people and young ones. Really? You are saying 'no'?"

"Well, I can tell you I'm not living with those venomous snakes ever! No, we are not helping and that is final. OH GOD!!!!!! Astar was in love with you Riel, did she cross the River Chebar? Did Astar repent?" Lazarus looked at Riel who nodded. He started hopping around again and couldn't even speak for his irritation. "RAHHHHHHHHH!"

Mini returned to her pocket perch. Riel stood up tall, crossed his arms and looked at Lazarus who started to storm off along with several his group. "Stop in your tracks. You owe me and my animals but more than that you owe Liam, who has freed you."

Suddenly a soft voice said, "So, Lazarus, are you sure your answer is NO? It seems to me that not long ago there was a man and his people begging me for mercy and to set his people free. Hummm...."

"I wonder about this Sloven. He has committed many sins, all of them very plain to me," said Liam stepping out from behind Riel.

The Freemen stopped and turned in disbelief. Many had never seen Liam and so some flung themselves to the ground. Lazarus still in a rage stood standing facing Liam with his arms crossed. They were about six feet apart and Lazarus had not regained his senses.

"I have never murdered," Lazarus yelled. "I've hurt no one without justification. I did not take the life of innocent children. I followed every rule and regulation you have all my life and for that I need to take in Eleeeeeegant? My answer is a definite no, Liam! You can't make me, and I will not do it. They murdered part of my own family, and I will not forgive them ever," sputtered Lazarus losing stream as he looked in Liam's luminous face.

"Okay Lazarus. When you were six do you remember stealing those jewels from your Aunty's chest, then lying to both your mother and father? Let's just skip to ten when you lied to your instructor, stole the other child's books, and then lied to everyone involved? You got an innocent party punished in that one?" Liam stepped forward lifted Lazarus onto a nearby rock, so their eyes were even with each other.

Lazarus crossed his arms, looked Liam in his face and said, "Those were very minor infractions and not even worthy of mention here!" Liam got even more luminous, and his eyes turned golden, his body emitting light. Lazarus knew he had over-stepped.

"You know it is a lengthy list and I really could go on for hours Lazarus," Liam said. "Fortunately, I love you. None of them are anything but sin and filthy rags in my sight. Sin has no depth or height; it is just sin! All of it. It is only because you have repented and accepted that you are less than perfect that I am here with you now. Riel has stood in front of thousands of Elegant setting you free and he did not know if he or Uriel, Fammy, Mini and Lawrence would survive. They all were willing to give their lives for your people. Yet when I come to you, your first words are 'no'?"

"All of my sin piled into a mountain could not come close to the sin in Astar's little finger," said Lazarus.

"No that is not truth Lazarus," said Liam. "Astar was never exposed or instructed in the love of God as you were. She had liars and murderers as her guides. It is only Riel's witness and his love for her that broke her bondage which was deeper than that of your own people. Would you care to see your sin even after you repented and started walking with me?" At that Liam, grabbed a near-by stick and started writing in the dust at Lazarus's feet.

Lazarus read some of what Liam wrote, turned bright red, and said, "Stop Liam, please stop. I can't bear this."

"Sin is sin," said Liam. "Even Riel who is a righteous man has sin. It is by mercy and grace alone that you stand before me in my presence because, long, long ago, I paid a price and covered you with my perfect, sinless nature so you could stand before my Father. I created you Lazarus to fulfill your part in the Prophecy. I command you now: You are to love Astar as your own daughter and do as Riel says and accept the repentant Elegant as your people."

"What of Astar? Where is the justice in this?" said Lazarus.

"The price for her sin and yours has been paid. The consequences of her transgressions still to come in her life.

You, on the other hand Lazarus, are just being stubborn," said Liam.

"I can't love her, I just can't. I see the whips and my children's faces if I look at her miserable face," Lazarus cried.

"Perhaps with a little time, and some sincere prayer, I can help you overcome this shortcoming." The double meaning of Liam's words was not lost on Riel or some in the crowd who half suppressed a laugh. "Lazarus, I didn't ask you to do the impossible. Astar can live with some of the other Freemen. You must help them get to here and take them to your new home with you. You must make your people understand and abide with this. Put into practice what you have learned, seen, or heard from me."

Lazarus started to respond by saying, "I guess I could live with her just near," when a burst of energy flashed, and Liam was gone. Lazarus fell flat over on his face and realized after a moment he was completely blind.

17

FREEDOM INDEED

*"Whatever you have learned, or received or heard from me,
or seen in me, put into practice
and the God of peace will be with you."*
Philippians 4:9

Three wagons were loaded with supplies, and several of the Freemen were sent back with extra horses. Lazarus, much to his chagrin, sat in a wagon bed to make the return journey. They assembled the day after Liam's visit and left late in the afternoon.

The weather had hints of autumn in the wind and the days were very pleasant but cool at night. The road was dry and the return uneventful. When Riel realized the Elegant camp was near, he halted the whole procession and had them wait under some spreading old oak trees. It was a chill wind that morning and Riel had to get his jacket from the pack. Now that he had Windring back, he knew the distance between would not take long. He summoned Lawrence and with Mini in his lap returned to the Elegant.

Uriel and Fammy met him a mile from camp. "Oh, are we glad to see you Riel," Fammy cried when she saw him. "A group of the Elegant have returned to the Citadel. I warned them that if they crossed back across the Chebar, they and their children could not return to the Freemen. But they did not want to eat berries or our biscuits and started several others complaining. Just think they didn't even have to move camp at all. Samuel helped us a lot and Miriam set up better ovens, but they walked off yesterday morning saying they wanted back with their friends and relatives. We lost a third of the camp."

Riel got down off Windring and ran over to Uriel and Fammy and put his arms around their necks. "I have missed you friends," he said with a catch in his throat. Mini jumped up between the ears of Uriel and kissed his forehead with her tiny lips. Uriel looked up cross-eyed. Riel said, "I am sorry those people left you. However, they are the weeds in the garden, to shrink or fail or be pulled from the true crop. This is not your fault if you tried."

"We tried everything, and Samuel even had a meeting the night before. He made sure that they understood what the consequences were. Astar made a speech and pleaded with them to no avail," remarked Uriel secretly glad for the return of Mini between his ears.

"Well, the Freemen are not happy, but they came to help. Actually, I was worried we did not have enough help with the original group, but I think it is manageable now. Lazarus had a visit from Liam in front of all of us and when he left in a blinding burst of light, Lazarus was blind. He is riding in a wagon behind us and did some talking to the Freemen to make them come. This is not going to be an easy introduction."

Fammy asked, "What should we do Riel?"

Riel had the bears and Mini return to the Freemen, and he rode into the Elegant camp.

He was surprised at the number that had left the night before. However, those who had stayed surrounded him and Windring with sounds of surprise and delight. "Prepare my people, the Freemen ride behind me and are here to help and move you to your new home," said Riel.

"Feel the crisp air this morning as you must move forward before the winter sets snow in your path. Though the way is hard the prize is waiting for you."

The next hours were filled with energy and expectation as the camp moved toward the Freemen. Although not far, Riel made them walk as he knew they would be hot, thirsty, and wanting when they arrived. The Freemen were still angry, but they had generous and merciful hearts. The last to arrive were the Mathematicians who had the assistance of Lawrence. Lawrence refused to let them ride on his back, but he did let them hold his tail or one of the saddlebag ties and he was very patient in encouraging their movement.

When Astar saw Lazarus, she ran to him, her hair tied in an unkempt knot, her face streaked with dirt, her clothes in shambles and bowed before the blind man. She touched his foot. "Forgive me for what I have done to you, your people, and your family. I want to honor you all the days of my life. Liam has saved me and set me free and now I pray for your vision to return. Forgive me, forgive us."

Lazarus eyes cleared the moment she said this to him, and he looked around in amazement. "I can see! I can SEE AGAIN!" This and the sorry state of the people arriving moved the Freemen's hearts to mercy. In the end, they had them all loaded up and moving after a fine meal and a drink of the stolen relished wine from the King's cellars the Freemen had brought back to encourage them. The wagons and extra horses took the bulk of them but that still left the two Mathematicians out.

This left them looking at the two bears whose glances at Riel told the whole story.

Uriel looking very unhappy said, "I told you I will not do it, Riel. It is already beyond my dignity to have done some of the things you wanted. I am not doing this and suffer with a bear bad back for years afterward."

Fammy joined with, "Sorry. Me either."

Riel scratched his head and walked a few feet away. He wasn't sure how to fix this when Lazarus walked back to him. "Oh, I see we have a LARGE, BIG and enormous problem I did not think about."

Just then Bully and Billy appeared with three other large cohort buffalos. Bully arrived and with a look of utter disgust said, "Now look, this is only because Liam asked us again and sent three more to help get these two mega mountain men to their home. We ain't doing the human thing traveling with you guys and need to make this as quick as possible so we are taking these two our own way and we are not waiting. Get them some food together and their night rolls and something to protect their nether region and we will get them to the destination."

"Winter is on the air this morning if you did not notice. We must get back to the herd and they are moving southwest as we speak. We thought about saying 'no' but Liam has always kept us and so we do this to honor him." The Mathematicians looked very frightened and scared. The bruises from the previous ride had just healed enough not to be painful.

Riel smiling said, "Bully, thank you for coming to us. We did not know what to do. But I want to extract a real promise from all five of you first."

"Oh, here it comes. Need I guess that you do not want the packages injured, maimed, rolled, bruised, bleeding, or beaten to a pulp like last time? That takes most of the excitement out of the prospect." He grinned exhibiting huge front teeth and nodded to the other buffalos standing by. They all guffawed and one jumped up a few inches but then they all settled down.

"Yes, you have indeed guessed what I want you to do," said Riel.

"Well guys, you promise to be tender loving buffalos to our esteemed and hugely honored guests? Emphasis on huge in that sentence." Bully chuckled and turned to the rest of them. They all promised.

"Bully? Bully?"

"Oh okay, I promise too. Dang it!"

With the help of the Freemen the buffalos were equipped and loaded. Bully groaned a lot, but Billy cried out when Elgenius was put on his back. This time the men had stirrups and reins. When all was ready, Bully said, "HI HO gang we are away!" The five of them took off in an arrow formation which was soon lost from sight in clouds of brown dust. The rest of the Elegant were watching and commenting that it still looked like a rough ride at the speed the buffalos were traveling.

Soon they were assembled into a wagon train. The people were all moving towards the lofty mountains with their new crowns of snow. Ten days later they found the Freemen who were not at all pleased that the Mathematicians had been dumped in their laps three days before. They had to allocate a wagon to each of the scholars and the food sacks had to be distributed on those riding horses to get them to the home grounds.

They found their new home a ten days later.

Four hundred years before, their own people were taken by the Elegant from this very spot. The remnants of buildings were still up against the overhanging cliffs, but the major find was the system of caves inside the mountain: A fresh clean deep-water lake was down below the main cavern, the ceiling in both places hundreds of feet above and the floor worn by the ancestor's feet to the point it was almost flat and shiny in many places. Shelves of rock dotted the circumference and one spot, with an interior and exterior exit, was obviously used as a stable with the dividers left intact. In front of the main entrance stretched a wide green lush meadow surrounded by tall pine trees.

Further below, at the end of the valley, obvious remnants of crop fields and abandoned buildings were a further boon. Towering granite mountains surrounded the valley bowl below. The Freemen would have to work hard to prepare for winter.

Two days later Riel stretched long and hard from his sleep. He knew he had to leave as his heart demanded. He began to prepare as soon as he got up.

Astar came to the creek where he was drying anything he needed to pack into his saddle bags. "Greetings, Riel," she said in a sunny happy voice. Then she looked around and realized the packs and saddle bags were out and he was preparing to leave.

"Hello Astar. As you can see, I must leave today. I know that Lazarus will take good care of you," said Riel.

"I am going with you Riel. I will go to prepare my things," said Astar.

"You will not do such a thing. You are spoiled, and no traveler as I have seen over the past week," said Riel.

"What do you mean saying that. I can ride a horse as well as any of the Freemen. I am worthy of your company, and I insist you take me," Astar replied.

"NO!"

"NO! You cannot tell me that. I'm going to get Lazarus."

Riel folded his clothing then loaded both Windring and Lawrence.

"You know she's hoping to cause you grief. You cannot let her come with us. She's off causing trouble even now," remarked the Lawrence. They looked at the group of Freemen and Elegant forming in front of the main cave.

"Lawrence, go get the bears for me. I have everything packed and we can leave after I talk to the people. Tell the bears to meet me at the far end of the Valley near the exit and you go with them. Here take Mini with you. Astar is NOT coming anywhere with me and distracting us." Mini jumped into the saddle on Lawrence's back. "Hurry, we have to leave as soon as possible."

Riel rode over to the pandemonium Astar had caused at the cave entrance and everyone quieted and looked at him. "I have had a command to go to the Desert people next. I must leave before any of your stubborn people try to follow or help me. I am to travel on my own with my animals. You are fine here in your beautiful new home and will have to work hard to make it through the winter with the Elegant, learning how to live without slaves. Believe it or not, I think the scholars might be of great help to you. They both have a kind of wisdom and Liam says to listen to their suggestions about crops and rotations. Lazarus, you must remain and not let anyone follow me. I ride hard and fast to beat the early snows coming." He pointedly looked at Astar who had Lazarus fix her hair that morning. Big tears formed in her dark eyes when he proclaimed:

"May God bless and keep each of you. I will return if it is in the Lord's will, but I know my journey has only just begun and this earth is full of evil. May the blessings of our Father rest on all of you. Astar, I do love you. Never forget that but live your life to the fullest as my journey may not allow me to return to you. Lazarus, be well and be blessed, look at the bounty God has delivered to your people."

All of them looked towards the end of the Valley and the sun rays bursting between the clouds. Riel's animals were halfway across, and a band of sunlight highlighted their departure. Riel spurred Windring but stopped a few hundred feet on and turned to wave. Everyone in the crowd was waving and shouting, Elegant and Freemen alike.

The End

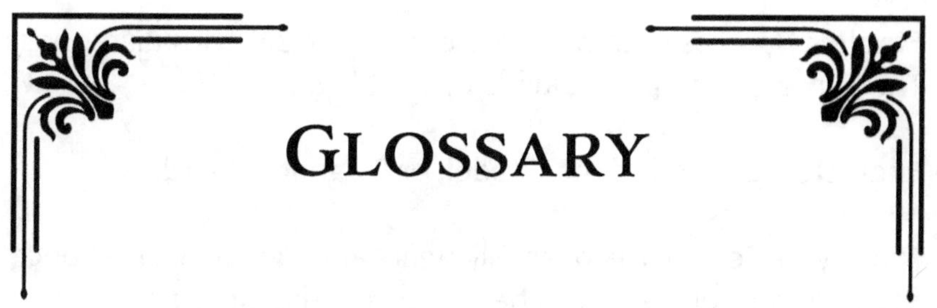

GLOSSARY

Adriel – Riel Ran Agam's mother, who died giving birth to him at the hand of Aragant. She was the true Queen of the Western Kingdom and was married to Agam the King.

Agam – The true King of the Western Kingdom. Father of Riel Ran Agam. Killed by Char La Tan and Aragant in a coup.

Astar – Elegant King Kester's only daughter.

Aragant – False King Char La Tan confidant and General.

Aristate – Sorcerer who assists King Char La Tan. His daughter sees the future and the past through a crystal.

Belial – Captain of King Char La Tan's bodyguard. Under General Aragant. Ran caravans for the King.

Billy – The first huge Buffalo required to transport the two Mathematicians to the Freemen's home.

Bully – The second huge buffalo transporting the Mathematicians.

Constantine – Belial's teacher in the Holy City.

Etharis –The first Mathematician for the Elegant.

Elgenius – The second Mathematician for the Elegant.

Etriele's Harness – Gold encrusted; filigree set with diamonds. The harness used by the Kings of the Elegant.

Enginele – General of the Citadel, or Elegant's guard.

Fammy – a Female Filk bear. Filk Bears are huge bears that once roamed the Northern Reaches. They are almost extinct.

Freeborn – a Silkie. Silkies are seals that can turn into women. Freeborn is one of the two Silkies that raised Riel.

Joshua – Sloven bath attendant to Riel.

Kruche – Port on the Carmel Coast. Where Liam and Riel went to start the journey.

Kester – King of the Elegant. Astar's Father.

Liberty – The second of two Silkies that raised Riel.

Le Moya – Sorcerer Aristate's mad daughter. She reads the past and future from a crystal.

Minions – Personal guards for Aragant.

Mount Moragan – Where the book of the Prophecy was found.

Milieus – A heavy gold coin that predicted the return of the True King.

Mini – Marmot sent by Liam to assist Riel at the White Lake.

Narky – The Carson Inn owner.

Riel Ran Agam – The true King of the Western Kingdom; Son of Queen Adriel and King Agam.

Ridel's Heart – A vial with Queen Adriel's blood which has magic properties to heal.

Samuel – Elegant Lieutenant who crosses the River Chebar and assists in getting the Freemen home.

Silkies – Female seals that have long lives and can turn into human women at will. However, it is very painful for them.

Windring – Riel's horse from King Kester's stables.

Windrider – Elegant King Kester's horse.

Uriel – Male Filk bear from the Northern Reaches.

ABOUT THE AUTHOR

Born at the base of the Rocky Mountains in a tiny town near Calgary, Alberta, Canada, Heather has loved the arts since was born. Her mother was an aspiring watercolor artist, and her father could craft almost anything with his hands. Since she was little, she has had a broad and prolific imagination.

She graduated from Evergreen Community College in 1988 as the Outstanding Graduate in English. From there, she opened a commercial business providing manuscripts, articles and stories in combination with professional photography to magazines and newspapers. She has been published numerous times over the years, but her goal was to write a book full of imagination, drama and values.

Drawing from various sources, she began to literally dream of the characters in this book. Over the years, the landscape and people, as well as the animals all came to life in her continuing dreams. Gifted in the fine arts field also, her oil, acrylic and pastel paintings are exhibited in four galleries in two states. She also does a number of shows all over the United States. Recognized by Master Signature status by Paint America, her life-like, realistic work has many awards and ribbons. The paintings and photographs in Come the Kingdom are all Heather's. Come the Kingdom is the culmination of her ability to bring the reader into a scene with finely detailed descriptions, colorful characters and the battle of good versus evil.